A new name and a new
attitude to match . . .

"Look, there's something you guys need to know about me," I said. "I'm always causing trouble. Trouble is my middle name." I said it like I believed it.

"I thought it was Delilah," said Amber.

"Nah, I was just kidding about that. JD really stands for Juvenile Delinquent!" They all laughed. I couldn't believe it. If getting in trouble got me this much attention, it was worth it. If I could keep this up all month, my personality makeover would be a huge success. It was only the first day, but already I felt more like JD than Judith.

One Summer. One Sleepaway Camp.
Three Thrilling Stories!

Summer Camp Secrets

How far will Kelly
go to hold on to
her new friends?

What happens when Judith
Ducksworth decides to
become JD at camp?

Can Darcy and
Nicole's friendship
survive the summer?

Summer Camp Secrets

ACTING OUT

by
Katy Grant

ALADDIN PAPERBACKS

New York   London   Toronto   Sydney

For my three favorite people—
Eric, Jackson, and Ethan.
You guys are my world.

ALADDIN PAPERBACKS
An imprint of Simon & Schuster Children's Publishing Division
1230 Avenue of the Americas, New York, NY 10020
Text copyright © 2008 by Katy Grant
All rights reserved, including the right of reproduction
in whole or in part in any form.
ALADDIN PAPERBACKS, *Summer Camp Secrets*, and
colophon are trademarks of Simon & Schuster, Inc.
Designed by Christopher Grassi
The text of this book was set in Perpetua.
Manufactured in the United States of America
First Aladdin Paperbacks edition May 2008
10 9 8 7 6 5 4 3 2 1
Library of Congress Control Number 2007935962
ISBN-13: 978-1-4169-3577-3
ISBN-10: 1-4169-3577-0

Acknowledgments

I am so grateful to Andréa Mendoza, who, as a recent Guard Start grad, let me interview her repeatedly, answered my many questions, and read the manuscript, offering me her advice. Her expertise and knowledge were an immense help as I wrote this book.

Also, thanks to Barbara Parsons, who read this manuscript and, as always, gave me sage advice, support, and insight. She is far more than a critique partner; she is a true friend.

And thanks to my gaming consultants—you know who you are.

CHAPTER 1

Sunday, June 15

This was it. I was about to leave my past behind me and start my new life. All I had to do was say good-bye to my family and get on the bus.

My mom clutched my arm. "Promise me you'll wear your headgear," she said, loud enough for twenty people to hear. Was that the most important thing she had to say to me before I left for a whole month?

"Mom! I told you I would. Stop asking me." We were in a huge crowd of parents and kids, all hugging and saying good-bye.

I looked around at the girls near me. One girl had on a ton of eye makeup, and she kept looking at her nails. They had that stupid white line painted across the top. The girl beside her was chatting away about something.

Another girl stood with her parents, not saying anything. She held a unicorn backpack in front of her like a shield.

"We'll e-mail you tomorrow to see how you're doing, but you'll have to write us back by snail mail, so I packed some envelopes and stamps for you," said Mom.

"Okay, thanks." I tried to sound grateful instead of annoyed, since she'd told me this three times already. She had her arm around me, and she wouldn't let go. It wasn't her fault she was being so clingy. This was my first time away from home.

"Gimme a hug, darlin'." Dad grabbed me away from Mom and squeezed my guts out. A couple of the other dads looked up at him. He's six foot four, so he's easy to spot in a crowd. "Have a great time. And don't worry about us. We can take care of ourselves."

I nodded but didn't say anything. I wished he hadn't said not to worry. How could I not? But maybe I'd have a break from worrying about my family for a while.

Then Adam hugged me. "Have fun, munchkin. Don't get eaten by a bear."

"I won't!" I laughed and hugged him back. He's fifteen, and he's already six foot one. I was going to miss being called munchkin. I felt small around my dad and brothers, but most of the time I felt like a giant freak, since I'm so tall for a girl. "Thanks for coming with us," I told him, but then I wished I hadn't said it. It made it sound like I was mad at Justin because he was still in bed when we left. I'd had to say good-bye to him at home.

"I guess I should go," I said. The bus engine was rumbling, and stinky gas fumes filled up the whole parking lot. Mom hugged me one more time and then finally let me go so I could get in line. I looked at the sign on the front of the bus. CAMP PINE HAVEN. Cool. My new life was about to begin.

I stood in line, smushed between girls in front of me and behind me. I kept my tennis racket pointed down so I wouldn't bop anyone in the knees. Somehow the girl with the unicorn backpack had ended up in front of me, only now the backpack was on her shoulders and pressed against my stomach.

I looked back at my family and waved before going up the steps. Mom smiled but she was blinking a lot, so I knew she was about to cry. Dad and Adam waved back.

We all shuffled down the bus aisle. Girls were cramming pillows, backpacks, and other junk in the overhead storage bins and holding up the whole line. By the time I made it halfway down the aisle, all the front seats were full. So what? I wanted to sit in the back anyway. I walked past the eye makeup girl and her friend, past the unicorn backpack, and was about to sit next to a girl with a long brown ponytail when she stuck her hand over the empty space and said, "It's taken."

The girl in the seat behind Ponytail said, "You can sit here."

"Thanks." I shoved my tennis racket and backpack in the overhead bin and plopped down in the seat next to her. She smiled at me. She was African American, and she had on little wire-rimmed glasses, a yellow tank top, and daisy earrings. She was really tiny. She probably didn't weigh more than seventy pounds dripping wet with rocks in her pockets.

"I'm Natasha."

"Hi," I said. She glanced at me like she was waiting for something. The bus was moving now, and the driver was trying not to mow down all the parents still standing in the parking lot.

"What's your name?" she asked finally.

That was an easy question. Ordinarily. Most people know the answer to that by the time they're two. I almost gave her the wrong name, out of habit. But then I remembered who I was supposed to be.

"JD. That's what everyone calls me," I heard myself saying.

It felt so strange to say my new name out loud. Now that I'd told one person, there was no turning back. I'd have to stick to my plan.

"Nice to meet you, JD." She cleared her throat. I could tell she was a little on the shy side, but I still liked her. "What does JD stand for?"

I stared at her like I was in a trance. What was I supposed to say to that? I thought I could just tell people to call me JD and they would. Did they have to know my whole boring life story?

I tried to think of something funny. "Just Dandy!" I said. It wasn't that funny, but it was better than the truth. Natasha looked at me like I was speaking Portuguese.

"Okay, I'm kidding. That's not what it stands for." I stalled, trying to think of a better answer. The bus made a wide turn and I gripped the seat in front of me to keep from sliding over and smashing Natasha against the window.

"You want to know what it really stands for? It's pretty embarrassing."

Natasha's eyes got bigger. "Oh, you don't have to tell me."

"No, I don't mind. My first name is January and my middle name is December. Crazy, huh? I have really weird parents. You know, the New Agey type. It could've been worse. At least they didn't name me Apple."

Natasha smiled, which made me feel bad about telling her such a goofy story. But it was part of the plan. I wanted to make sure no one at camp ever knew my real name.

Judith Duckworth. I've always hated my name. It thounds like I'm lithping when I thay it. Mom named me after her grandmother. She was crazy about her grandmother, and she thought naming me after her would be a great way to honor her. Too bad my great-grandma's name wasn't Ashley.

I'd never told anyone to call me JD before, but that was about to change. I'd tried to come up with some kind of nickname for myself, but I didn't want Judy— that sounded old to me—and Ducky was even worse. I figured initials would be pretty good. And I liked the way they sounded. JD. That was *sooo* much better than Judith. Already my life was improving.

Natasha looked at me. "Are you nervous about going to camp?"

"No. Why should I be? I think it'll be fun."

She smiled and scooted her glasses up on her nose.

"You're braver than I am. I'm nervous about meeting a lot of new people."

"You know what my dad said about going someplace where nobody knows you? He said I should think of it as a fresh start."

Natasha nodded like that made a lot of sense. My dad also said camp would give me a break from all the stuff our family has been through, but I didn't mention that.

A fresh start. That was what I was most looking forward to. Going someplace where nobody knew me.

Fifth grade was when I first realized how boring I was. That was the year Chloe Carlson came to our school. You'd think being the new girl would be hard, but it wasn't for this girl. From Day One all the boys were in love with her and all the girls wanted to be her friend. Part of it was her name. How could you be anything but cool with a name like Chloe Carlson? Her parents obviously knew what they were doing. They didn't name her something random like Bernice. Or Judith.

This year, in sixth grade, I tried to act like Chloe. I made funny comments in class and I tried to be everyone's friend, but it didn't really work. Everybody stared at me and said, "Why are you acting so weird?"

So when my dad said camp would be a fresh start, I figured it was time for a personality makeover. Then I had this great idea. I'd borrow Chloe's personality while I was away at this summer camp in North Carolina, and she'd never even have to know.

While I talked to Natasha, I tried to think what Chloe would do if she was on this bus right now. She'd say something funny loud enough for everyone to hear. I just wasn't sure what that funny thing would be.

"Do you have any brothers or sisters?" asked Natasha. Now the bus was making a humming noise, and everyone was pretty quiet, talking to the people next to them.

I thought about it for a second. I could tell her anything—make up an older sister or a baby brother. But I decided to go with the truth. I didn't want to act like Justin and Adam didn't exist. "Yeah. Two brothers. Both older. What about you?" At least I could tell her that and she wouldn't say, *Oh the football stars at Central High? THEY'RE your brothers?*

"I'm an only child."

"Really? What's that like?"

Natasha shrugged. "Okay, I guess. It's all I know. I think that's why my parents are sending me to camp. So I can see what it's like to live with other kids for a change. But I'm really going to miss them. The three of us are very close."

"Hey, we've got a whole month without parents," I said. "It'll be great." Then I did the craziest thing I've ever done in my life. I stood up and yelled really loud, "Hey, everyone, let's hear it for a whole month without parents!" Then I whooped, the way I would at Justin's and Adam's football games. "Woo-hoo! Woo-hoo!"

When everyone turned and stared at me, I smiled and waved, like I was glad to be making a fool of myself. Then I slid back down in the seat. Natasha's eyebrows were way above the rims of her glasses.

"Sorry. Didn't mean to cause a scene," I told her. I could tell she hadn't expected me to do that. *I* hadn't even expected me to do that. Chloe wouldn't have done something *that* stupid. I hoped I wasn't blushing. It felt weird being the center of attention—like I was wearing someone else's shoes instead of mine. It didn't seem to fit right.

"It's just that this bus ride is pretty boring, don't you think?" I asked Natasha, acting like I was used to being the life of the party. "I mean, look at everyone. They're all half-asleep. We should liven this place up. I know! Let's sing 'A Hundred Bottles of Beer on the Wall'! Everyone loves that song!" Maybe the more I acted this way, the faster I'd get used to my new self.

"No, they don't," said the ponytail girl in the seat in

front of us. "Why don't you do us all a favor and shut up?" she added over the back of her seat. The friend she'd saved a seat for turned around and gave me a dirty look too.

I had no idea what to say to that. For one thing, nobody would ever tell Chloe Carlson to shut up while she was being funny. And if anyone ever said anything slightly sarcastic to her, she always had a quick comeback. Always. I tried to think of something, but my brain was frozen.

The ponytail girl had turned back around. She figured she'd shut me up for good. I did feel pretty silly. I wasn't very good at acting this way. I felt like covering my face with my hands, so I did, but then I got inspired.

I sat there with my face covered up and pretended to cry. I let out these loud *boo-hoo* sounds. "I don't have any friends!" I sobbed, loud enough for everyone around me to hear. Then I looked up at Natasha. "Will you be my friend if I pay you a buck?"

That's when the girls behind me started to laugh. "I'll be your friend for five bucks!" somebody yelled.

"Twenty for me!"

Natasha shook her head and grinned. "I had no idea I was inviting a crazy person to sit beside me. JD, of course I'll be your friend, and you don't need to pay me a dollar." She looked over the back of the seat. "I'll do it for free!" she said.

"My first friend!" I yelled. "I actually have a friend now!" The two girls in front of us had put their pillows over the tops of their heads to cover up their ears. "And I've got some enemies, too!" I shouted.

Natasha cracked up laughing. I could only imagine what my friends back home would've said. *Judith, what's wrong with you? You never act like this.*

Maybe Judith didn't. But JD did.

CHAPTER 2

"We're finally here!" said Natasha when we turned onto a gravel road and passed a sign that said CAMP PINE HAVEN FOR GIRLS. She jiggled her knee up and down as she looked out the window. We passed a lake and some tennis courts. There were tons of people all around and a lot of cars lined up along the road.

When we got off the bus, a bunch of counselors were waiting for us and yelling directions. They all had on matching green shirts, so they were easy to spot. They broke us up into age groups, and Natasha and I found out we were both in the group called Middlers—ages ten to twelve. That made us the oldest in the group.

Then a lady with a clipboard asked us our names. When it was my turn, I said, "JD Duckworth," like I'd always been called that. She looked at her list and didn't seem at all confused. "Okay, JD. You're in Middler Cabin Two A."

Then Natasha said, "Natasha Cox."

"Hi, Natasha. You're in Middler Cabin Three B."

Natasha and I looked at each other. "Can't we switch? We're best friends. We really need to be together," I said.

The lady shook her head. "Sorry, cabin assignments have already been made. But you'll still see a lot of each other." She smiled and moved on to the next girl.

Natasha and I walked over to where all the luggage from the bus was piled up. "I can't believe it. We just get to know each other and we're already split up," I said.

Natasha pushed her glasses up her nose. Now that I was standing next to her, I saw that she only came up to my shoulder. "I know, but like she said, we'll still see each other a lot."

Some guys wearing red T-shirts that said "Camp Crockett" helped us carry our trunks to the cabins. It was weird that the camp made everyone bring trunks to keep all their stuff in, but that's what the letter had said to do. Plus they gave us a list of what to bring and told us to put name tags in all our clothes. When my mom was getting my things ready, I felt like I'd joined the army.

We had to climb up a big hill to get to where the cabins were. I was glad I only had to carry my tennis racket and backpack.

"It sure is pretty here, isn't it?" asked Natasha. It was a sunny day, and everything was so green. There were trees everywhere, big rock formations, lots of hills, and off in the distance, bluish-colored mountains. All the buildings were wooden, and the whole camp looked like it should be on a postcard or something.

At the top of the hill we came to a long row of cabins. "Well, I guess this is good-bye—for now," said Natasha when we got to the door of Cabin 2. She looked scared.

"Okay. I'll see you later." It was too bad we couldn't stay together.

The guys carried my trunk in and left it inside. When I walked in, a counselor with curly blond hair said, "Hey! Are you my camper? I'm Michelle!"

She was obviously a counselor because she looked older, and she was wearing one of those green shirts, but I was about three inches taller than she was. I'm five foot six, and my doctor says I'm still growing. If I keep growing till I'm eighteen, I figure I'll be six-nine eventually.

"I'm JD. JD Duckworth."

She frowned a little like she'd never heard of me, but then she said, "Oh, okay. Nice to meet you, JD!" She had a great grin that made her eyes crinkle up.

The cabin was awesome. It had screens all around it, so it felt really open and breezy. And there were bunk beds. I've always wanted bunk beds. Justin and Adam had them a long time ago, but they each have their own room now.

"This is cool," I said, looking around at everything. The walls and floors were wooden, and girls had written their names all over the place.

"Wow! 1981!" I yelled. I pointed to a spot on the wall that said JENNIFER H. 1981. "That is so amazing! These cabins are that old?"

Michelle laughed. "Yeah. And guess what? My mom went here when she was a kid. And some people have grandmothers who went here. Can you believe it?" Her eyes crinkled again. "I'll send my daughter here too—if I have one."

Two other girls were already in the cabin, and while we were all trying to get everyone's names straight, another girl came in.

"Here. These will help us get to know each other faster," said Michelle. She handed out name tags. They were made out of little round slices of wood with a plastic string, but when I saw mine, I almost had a heart attack. It had JUDITH written on it. So much for keeping my old name a secret.

I held it against my stomach. "I need a new one. One that says 'JD.'"

"No problem! I'll just change the old one." Michelle took a marker from a shelf beside her bed and wrote "JD" in big red letters on the back of the piece of wood. Then she hung the string around my neck with the "JD" side showing. "How's that?"

"Good. But can I see the marker for a second?" I asked. I took off my name tag, scribbled over JUDITH so no one could read it, and then put it back on again.

All the other girls were watching me, but I didn't care. I was officially JD now.

"What's your real name?" asked one girl.

"Josephina Delilah," I said, coming up with the weirdest name I could think of. "Terrible, huh? That's why I go by JD." Michelle smiled, and I knew she wouldn't give away my secret. Having initials as a name would be fun. I needed to think up lots of crazy names to tell people when they asked me what JD stood for. It would add to the mystery if nobody ever knew for sure.

Off in the distance we heard a bell ringing, and Michelle called out, "Hey, that means it's time for lunch.

Everybody follow me, and I'll show you where the dining hall is."

A lot of parents were still wandering around, and I sort of wished my parents could've seen the camp, but I was glad I'd taken the bus. I never would've gotten rid of my mom. I kept my eye out for Natasha till I spotted her walking with a group of girls. "Hey, let's sit together at lunch!"

"JD! I was looking all over for you. How do you like your cabin?"

"I love it, and I've got a great counselor. She's really friendly." It was so exciting to see the whole camp. I loved how woodsy and outdoorsy everything looked.

"Yeah, I like mine, too." She leaned close to me. "I'm not as nervous now."

I patted her back. "See, I told you this would be a fresh start."

But when we got inside the dining hall, we found out we couldn't sit together because we had to sit with all the people from our cabin. Michelle took me and the other girls to our table and introduced us to Alex, the counselor in Cabin 2B. She had deep blue eyes and light brown hair pinned up off the back of her neck. She was really pretty, but she didn't smile at all, so I was glad I was on Michelle's side of the cabin.

"Welcome to *Pain* Haven," said a girl with her elbows propped on the table and a sneer on her face. Her name tag said KATHERINE. "For all you new campers: This place bites. I've been coming here since I was seven. I should know."

"Nice," Alex said, frowning at her. "Maybe they'd like to decide for themselves." She looked at the rest of us. "I've been coming here since I was eleven. It's a great camp. I'm on the swimming staff."

"I'm canoeing, by the way," said Michelle, waving and smiling from the end of the table. "Katherine! We're going to have a terrific summer!"

Katherine rolled her eyes. "Whatever."

Lunch was great—tacos and fruit salad. I'd always heard that camp food was lousy, but I ate three tacos, and they didn't kill me. They didn't even make me queasy.

After lunch, Michelle pointed out different things as we walked back to the cabin. She said the oldest girls were called Seniors and the youngest were Juniors. We were right in the middle. "That's the camp office, and behind it is the infirmary, where the nurse is. That's the Crafts Cabin, and the stables are down that road."

One weird thing was the bathrooms. They weren't inside the cabins; instead there was a building called

Solitary with a bunch of sinks and toilets in it, and there was another outdoor building for the showers. It had a roof and shower stalls, but it was still like you were showering almost directly outside. I felt like we were really going to be camping out for the whole summer, and that would definitely be fun.

Back in the cabin, Michelle told us to pick out which beds we wanted. The cabin had two big rooms, A and B. Four of us were on Side A, and Alex was in charge of four girls on Side B. Luckily, Katherine was on her side of the cabin.

"I'll take a top bunk if nobody else wants one," I said. I'd been hoping for the top as soon as I saw the bunk beds.

"Then I'll take a bottom," said Courtney. Her hair was the first thing I'd noticed about her. It was hard not to. Here was this tiny person with a head of honey-colored hair so thick and wavy it looked like a lion's mane. She unpacked some sheets and started making up the bottom bunk below me.

"I guess I'll take the other top," said Lauren. Her blond hair was practically white, and she wore it in a short ponytail. The back of her shorts said "Dancer."

Amber, a girl with long brown hair and a nose that looked squashed, took the other bottom bunk. "This is my third summer, so let me know if you guys have any questions." She had a sweet smile, so I felt bad for thinking of her as the flat-nosed girl.

"Well, it's my first year, but I made one friend on the bus. She didn't want to be friends at first, till I paid her a buck. Oh, and I made several enemies, too!" I said. I realized I was talking too loud.

"How?" asked Amber, her forehead wrinkling.

"Just by being me!" I told her. I felt like I was auditioning for a play. I had to make a big impression so I'd get the part. The others looked at me like they didn't know what to think. Everyone started making up their beds. Was I ever going to pull this off? Did they think I was funny or just obnoxious?

I opened my trunk to get out my sheets, and the first thing I saw was my headgear on top, with a note from my mom. *Hi, sweetie! Remember: 14 hours a day! Love, Mom.*

Groan. At least she didn't call me Judith. Most of those hours were at night, but I had to put the thing on in the evening, and then I'd take it off when I woke up. I wished I could go the whole month without wearing it, but I'd probably go home and find out my teeth were permanently crooked. My cousin had such a bad bite, she had to have her jaw broken and then wired back together again.

So then, just to be stupid, I took out my head-gear and put it on, in front of everyone. I fluffed up my hair and declared, "Don't hate me because I'm beautiful!"

Luckily, everyone laughed, including Michelle.

"Do you only wear it at night?" asked Courtney from her bottom bunk, looking at me sympathetically.

"Mostly. My orthodontist calls me 'Beaver Face.' I'm his favorite patient."

Again I got laughs, so I figured I'd keep the stupid thing on for a while. I would never have let anyone see me in this back home. I'd been wearing it since February, and I'd missed Elise Rutherford's sleepover because my mom called her mom and told her to make sure I wore it. I pretended I had the flu.

"This is great! You guys are already getting to know each other!" said Michelle, watching us all as she sat cross-legged on her cot against the wall. Over on Side B, Alex's group was hardly talking at all.

Mom had carefully packed my trunk, but she'd put my sheets and towels at the very bottom. I piled a bunch of clothes and stuff on the floor beside me, trying to find the new striped sheets she'd bought for me.

"Oh, are those pictures from home? Can I see?" asked Michelle.

I looked down and saw my photo album peeking out from under my pile of stuff on the floor.

"Um, sure," I told her. What else could I say, now that she'd seen it? I handed the album to her and hoped she'd look through it and then give it back. The less everyone knew about my family, the better. I unfolded my sheets and climbed up to the top bunk to make my bed.

"Who are these guys? Are they your brothers?" she asked, flipping through the pages. I glanced down and saw that she was looking at Justin's and Adam's football pictures.

"Uh, yeah. They both play football," I said, deciding to leave it at that. I was wrestling with the sheets, so it was easy to act distracted.

"What positions do they play?"

From the top bunk, I could see the newspaper articles I'd cut out and pasted inside. One had a picture of Justin jumping up to catch a pass, and another had a picture of both of them together. I'd been so proud of them when those pictures were in the paper.

I climbed down and sat on the edge of Michelle's cot.

"That's Adam. He's fifteen, and he's a safety. He'll be on the junior varsity squad next year. And Justin's seventeen. He's a tight end." I could tell her a little about them. She didn't have to know *everything*.

Michelle read the headline. "'Central High Brothers Both Powerhouse Players.' Such cuties!" she said, even though they looked all sweaty and grimy in the picture.

"Do you like football?" I asked.

"Uh, that would be *yes*. I guess I didn't tell you where I go to college." She jumped up and pulled out an Oklahoma Sooners T-shirt from her trunk.

"Oh wow, great football school. Did you go to any games last year?"

"Every home game. I had season tickets. So I bet these guys will be getting football scholarships, huh?" she said with a big grin.

I shrugged. "Maybe." I just wanted to get off the subject of my brothers and football. I hadn't planned on telling anyone about that stuff.

"Maybe? Don't be modest." She nudged me with her elbow. "They're obviously both talented. They may be the next Manning brothers!"

I shook my head. "I wouldn't go that far. Anyway, they're not quarterbacks."

"Manning brothers?" asked Courtney. Michelle winked at me and grinned.

"You know—Peyton and Eli. They're both NFL quarterbacks." I wondered if I should tell her what "NFL" stood for. Who hadn't heard of the Manning brothers?

Just a few months ago my family did joke around about how maybe one day the boys would both be playing in the NFL, but nobody said that anymore. Not since what had happened this spring.

A bell rang and Michelle told us that now we all had to go to the lake to take swim tests. Everyone pulled swimsuits out of their trunks and started changing.

I was glad I could finally put my photo album away. I stuck it under a bunch of clothes at the bottom of my trunk. Why'd I even bring it along in the first place? I thought I'd want to look at it if I missed my family. But I could already tell I wasn't going to miss them that much. I had a whole month away from them, and I wanted to make the best of it.

I took off my headgear and found my new red one-piece in my trunk. I never wore bikinis because they made me look like a cow.

I really wanted my JD plan to work. So far, so good. But I had to make a big first impression. By the end of the day, I wanted a lot of people to know me. I still remembered Chloe's first day at my school. Everyone had said, "Have you met the new girl?" Now all I needed to do was to get everyone at this camp talking about the girl named JD.

The tough part was figuring out exactly how to do that.

CHAPTER 3

Michelle took all the Cabin 2 campers down to the lake together. Alex had left early since she was on the swim staff. Besides Katherine (or Miss Sunshine, as I silently thought of her), the other Side B girls were Mei, Isabel, and Meredith.

I looked at Mei's name tag and called her "Mee," but she said it was pronounced "May," like the month. She was Asian, but when her parents were helping her carry all her stuff into the cabin, I'd noticed they were both Caucasian, so I figured she was adopted.

Isabel had dark frizzy hair and freckles on practically every inch of her body. At lunch Meredith didn't eat the tacos because she was a vegetarian. She knew Michelle from last year, and she talked to her the whole time about canoeing.

I kept my eye out for Natasha, but I didn't see her anywhere. I looked at all the Cabin 2 girls, and they seemed pretty okay. Except for Katherine, who complained about how she'd done this stupid swim test every year.

"Great! It'll be easy for you," Michelle said, putting an arm around her shoulders.

Katherine wriggled away. "I hope I drown."

Of all the girls, Amber seemed most my type, or *Judith's* type—quiet but friendly, and a little . . . well, blah. If we'd met at school last year, we probably would've been best friends. Courtney, on the other hand, reminded me of Chloe Carlson. She was cute and bubbly like Chloe, but so far she didn't seem to have a killer sense of humor like Chloe, which was good. If she and I got to be friends, we couldn't both be cracking jokes all the time. I scooted up so I could walk close to her.

When we got to the lake, Michelle took off to say hi to some old friends, and we all sat down around the edge to wait our turn. Lots of girls were already waiting. A wooden dock jutted out over the lake, and Alex was standing at the end of it in a blue-and-white striped bikini, holding a clipboard and watching some girls in the water.

The test looked supereasy. We just had to jump in, tread water for five minutes, and then swim across the lake. And the lake wasn't very big, so it wouldn't be tough swimming across it. I figured it was maybe forty or fifty yards to the other side.

While the other girls talked, I thought about how Chloe would make some funny remark right now and crack everyone up. But I had one big problem. Chloe was naturally funny. I wasn't. It was like being born color-blind, or having one leg shorter than the other. I had a humor deficiency. Sure, it made things tougher, but that meant I had to try harder.

I stared at the water, trying to think of something funny to say. A group of girls dove off the end of the dock and started treading water. I could see some tiny things swimming around near the edge of the lake. At first I thought they were fish, but they didn't have tails. They were little dark blobs darting around in the water. Oh, they were tadpoles.

I jumped to my feet. "Shark! Shark!" I yelled at the top of my lungs. When everyone looked at me, I shrugged and sat down. "Oops! Sorry. It's just a stick. My bad."

It seemed like one of those moments on TV when everything freezes. All of a sudden about a hundred eyes were all looking at me. My heart thumped in my chest. I wished I could take it back. I felt so silly. How could funny people stand this kind of attention?

Alex blew her whistle and made the girls in the water swim up to the dock and climb out. Then she spun around and marched over to us. The other swim counselors had turned around to look at us too.

"WHO SAID THAT?" The sun was behind her back, and as she hovered over us, all we could see was this dark shadow.

Nobody said a word. Not one person was going to tell on me. *That* was pretty cool. I'd never done anything to purposely get in trouble before, and I couldn't believe that all these strange girls I'd just met already had my back.

"I asked you all a question. I know the girl who yelled that was sitting over here." The shadow leaned over us, and now we could see Alex's face, all dark and scary. "If I don't find out who it was, every one of my little Cabin 2 campers will swim an extra lap across the lake."

I had no idea what would happen next. There was a long silence while Alex waited for someone to say something. Amazing! They still wouldn't tell on me.

So that was when I did it. I crossed my arms and pointed at Lauren on one side of me and Courtney on the other. "I did it," I said, but I still pointed at the two of them. I heard Courtney let out a puff of air.

"Okay," said Alex, in a *now we're getting somewhere* tone. "So you're the wise guy. You think water safety is something to laugh at?"

She was being so lecturey, I couldn't stop myself. I held my hand over my eyes to shade them from the sun, and I threw her a salute and said, "Yes, Sergeant, I do think water safety is something to laugh at. I laugh at water safety every single day."

My heart would not stop pounding. I'd never been a smart mouth before in my whole life. It felt like jumping out of a plane. It was scary and exhilarating, and I didn't know how I was going to land.

Alex stood over me, staring me down. I could hear someone behind me trying not to giggle. "We'll see how funny it is. On your feet. You'll take your test now. And you'll swim two laps across the lake instead of one."

She led me over to where the other girls were standing on the end of the dock. They were all dripping wet, watching Alex yell at me, and I felt bad for making them stand there, because a couple of them were shivering.

I turned to look at the others sitting by the lake edge. I made a funny face behind Alex's back to show I didn't mind getting in trouble, and Courtney gave me a tiny, two-fingered wave. I was a little scared, but I'd definitely gotten noticed.

"Okay, ladies, this comedian is the one who interrupted your swim test. Apologize to these girls for making them stand here and wait."

I looked at all the girls dripping there on the end of the dock. "I'm vewy sowy I intewupted yowah swim test. Pwease fowgive me," I said. A couple of them had to hold back smiles.

What could Alex do to me? She looked at me like she wanted to drown me, but instead she yelled, "In the water!" and blew her whistle right in my ear.

I dove off the end of the dock, mainly to get away from that whistle. The water was icy cold, but when I came up for air, I started treading water right away, to warm myself up. The more I moved, the less cold I felt. Alex timed us with her watch. When five minutes were up, she told us all to swim across the lake. "Two for you," she said, pointing at me. "And if you cause any more trouble, we'll make it three."

I put my face down and started doing the crawl stroke. I was glad to be in the water now, out of the center of attention. I wasn't sure I could think up anything else funny to do. So I had to swim an extra lap. So what? There were worse ways to be punished. I figured

I'd do them really fast to show her I didn't care.

I kept my head down and breathed on every fourth stroke, the way Justin had taught me. Every now and then I'd look up to see how close I was. Pretty soon I'd made it to the other side, where another counselor with a clipboard was waiting on the edge of the lake. She smiled at me when I came up for air. She probably hadn't heard all the trouble I'd caused on the other side.

"Wow, you are some swimmer," she said. "Look at the rest of your group!"

I looked back, and the other girls were barely halfway across. I didn't know I'd gone *that* fast.

"Are you on a swim team in your hometown?"

"Nope. I've just always been a pretty good swimmer." I flipped my hair out of my eyes.

"You should think about taking the Guard Start class. It's for really good swimmers who aren't old enough to start actual lifeguard training. Think you'd be interested?"

"I don't know. Maybe." I'd never thought about being a lifeguard. I didn't really want to take any swimming classes. What I wanted to do this summer was get good at tennis, but she was being so nice to me, I figured I should at least act interested.

"What's your name and cabin number?" she asked.

"JD Duckworth, Middler 2A."

She flipped through some pages till she found my name and put a check mark next to it. "Okay, JD. I'm Libby. You passed the test with flying colors. And give the Guard Start class some thought. Classes begin tomorrow."

She sure was a lot nicer than Alex. "Will you be teaching it?" I asked.

"No, but don't worry. One of us on the swim staff will be."

She told me I could get out and dry off, but I said I had to do one more lap. "I was goofing around before the test, and Alex got a little mad."

Libby smiled at me. "Well, that shouldn't be a problem for you." I took off across the lake again, going even faster this time. Partly it was to get back at Alex, but partly I was showing off. Even if I didn't do the class, it was still pretty cool that she was amazed by my awesome swimming skills.

By the time I made it across the lake, the Cabin 2 girls were just jumping in for their test. I climbed the ladder at the end of the dock and shook myself off. Alex kept her eyes on the girls in the water. "Can I go now?" I asked, trying to be polite. I'd caused enough trouble for a while. She nodded and didn't look at me.

I was walking away to get my towel when she blew

her whistle. I thought she was after me again, but when I turned around, she was on her knees, yelling at someone. "Are you okay? Do you need the flotation?"

Now everyone was rushing over to see what was going on.

"Everyone out of the water!" Alex yelled. I could see one girl trying to keep her head above water, but she was definitely panicking. She went under and came up again, coughing like crazy. It was Isabel, the quiet one on Side B. The rest of the girls climbed up the ladder at the end of the dock, one by one, watching Isabel the whole time.

"Girls, move it!" yelled another counselor. She'd run up with this big red foam thing and she tossed it to Alex, who threw it out to Isabel. By now, everybody at the lake was watching.

Isabel grabbed the floaty thing, and Alex pulled her over to the dock. Then she grabbed her under the arms and sat her on the edge of the dock. Isabel sat there and coughed while Alex leaned over her. "Why'd you jump in if you can't swim? You should've told me you can't swim!" she shouted.

It took every ounce of energy I had to keep from running over to Alex and pushing her into the lake. How could she be so mean? It was bad enough that the poor kid had to be rescued, but did she have to embarrass her in front of everyone? Poor Isabel.

Alex turned around, and her face was as white as a new pair of gym socks. She looked pretty freaked out, but that still didn't give her the right to yell at Isabel.

Katherine had her hand over her mouth, snickering. "What a loser!" she said to Mei.

"Shut up, or I'll push you in," Mei hissed at her. I liked that girl. She was tiny, but she had the personality of a firecracker.

I wrapped myself up in my towel, then sat down on a big rock to wait for the other girls to finish. I finally saw Natasha, sitting about twenty feet away with the girls from her cabin. Isabel came and sat beside me on the rock. She wouldn't look at me.

"Don't worry about it," I told her. "Just shake it off."

Isabel nodded but kept staring at her toenails.

When the other girls finished their test, we all walked back to the cabin together.

"Wow! You were amazing," said Amber. "Way to show up Alex!"

"I told you I made enemies on the bus. Looks like I've made one more!"

"Thank you so much for admitting you were the one who yelled that," Lauren said. "I thought she was going to bust all of us." Her blond hair looked even whiter when it was wet and the sun was shining on it.

"Look, there's something you guys need to know about me," I explained. "I'm always causing trouble. Trouble is my middle name." I said it like I believed it.

"I thought it was Delilah," said Amber.

"Nah, I was just kidding about that. JD really stands for Juvenile Delinquent!" They all laughed. I couldn't believe it. If getting in trouble got me this much attention, it was worth it. If I could keep this up all month, my personality makeover would be a huge success. It was only the first day, but already I felt more like JD than Judith.

CHAPTER 4

Monday, June 16

"Prevention, fitness, response, leadership, professionalism." Alex held up one finger at a time and ticked off the five areas she wanted us to remember. "Those five areas will be our focus for the next four weeks."

Off in the shallow end I watched the nice counselor Libby with her advanced beginner class, working on back floats. They were mostly Juniors, eight or nine years old, and then poor Isabel, stuck with all the little kids. Isabel had been so embarrassed about having to be rescued yesterday, but right now I wished I could switch places with her.

There was a long silence, and I looked up to see why Alex had stopped talking. She stared at me with her arms crossed, and the rest of the class was looking at me too.

"Do I have your undivided attention now?" snarled Alex. I nodded and wrapped my towel more tightly around my shoulders. Boy, she really hated me, but the feeling was completely mutual. I almost died when I found out *she* was teaching the Guard Start class. Why couldn't it have been Libby?

Alex kept talking and I tried to listen. Six of us had signed up for the class, and I was glad that most of them were from my cabin: Courtney, Mei, and Lauren. Besides us there were two other girls, Claudia and Shelby. We were all huddled up with our towels wrapped around us like blankets. It was only nine thirty, and it was freezing out here. Okay, maybe not quite freezing, but it was probably in the sixties at least. When we woke up this morning, the cabin felt like a refrigerator, and we'd all worn jackets and sweats to breakfast. I had no idea the mountains got so cold at night.

"I have to warn you that the final test will be really demanding," said Alex. "You'll have to tread water for two minutes without using your hands, swim five hundred yards without stopping, and retrieve a ten-pound object from a depth of ten feet."

Courtney poked me in the ribs, and I glanced at her. Her eyes widened, and I raised my eyebrows. It did sound pretty hard. Five hundred yards—that was like swimming five football fields.

"I have another Guard Start class with Senior girls who are thirteen and fourteen, but most of you are twelve. So you're all a little young." She paced back and forth and locked her eyes on each one of us as she talked. "I fully expect that some of you won't be able to hack it, and you'll drop out. A few of you might get all the way through the class, but maybe you won't pass the final test. If you do pass, your next step will be taking a lifeguarding class when you're fifteen." She stopped in front of us and crossed her arms.

"You'll also be expected to complete thirty service hours—helping out with swimming lessons for the little kids. So this class is going to be a lot of hard work. Anyone who's not ready to give it her all should leave now."

I jumped to my feet and waved to everyone. "I guess this is good-bye! Have fun!"

Alex stepped aside to let me pass, but I felt someone yank my towel from behind. It was Courtney. "She's just kidding." She and Lauren pulled me down and made me sit between them. Courtney held on to my towel like she didn't trust me to sit still.

I could have easily walked away. Who needed this?

I didn't even want to be a lifeguard, so this class was a complete waste of time for me. I'd wanted to go to the climbing tower this morning, but Courtney and Lauren had dragged me here instead. They thought the class sounded cool, and then Mei wanted to do it too. So I came along, mostly to be with them. They seemed like the type of girls Chloe would be friends with.

Alex was staring me down. "You're welcome to go. Why don't you leave now before you waste another minute of my time?" Courtney gripped my towel tighter, so I kept quiet and didn't move.

"Are you staying or going?" Alex asked, boring a hole through me with her blue death-ray eyes.

I shrugged. "I might as well stay. I'm dressed for the part." I opened and closed my towel really fast. Mei bit the edge of her towel to keep from smiling. Alex turned away and started blabbing about the five areas again.

It felt scary being the troublemaker. But if I was going to try this out, camp was definitely the place to do it. I'd thought about it a lot since Alex had yelled at me yesterday. What could she do to me? What could any of the counselors do to me? It wasn't like school, where you got called to the principal, or got detention, or got a note sent home to your parents. The worst thing they could do to me was send me home, but I'd have to do something major, like set the cabin on fire, to have *that* for a punishment. And I wanted to be a comedian, not an arsonist.

When Alex finished jabbering, she gave us all workbooks, and we did exercises in them called "Safety First" and "Know Your PFD: Personal Flotation Device." Then she told us all to get into the water to swim laps. "Four laps, ladies. Across the lake and back, two times." Then she pointed to me and said, "JD's doing five laps today. Just to show me how committed she is to the class."

Alex blew her whistle and we lined up to dive in. I went second after Lauren, and when I came up for air I was gasping from the cold.

"How is it?" asked Mei from the dock, her arms folded across her chest and her shoulders hunched. If she was cold now, the water was really going to wake her up.

"Fr-freezing!" I yelled. The water was so frigid it made my head ache.

"Colder than yesterday?" asked Courtney.

"Yes!" Lauren and I shouted at the same time.

Alex blew her whistle at us. "Stop complaining and start swimming!" One by one, the others dove in. After everybody had screamed and groaned and gotten over the shock, we all started across the lake.

"I'm never going to make it," said Courtney when she came up for air. Her teeth chattered, and her lips were pale.

"Sure you will. It's not that far," I told her.

"No, I mean everything. This class. There's no way I'll ever pass it."

"Me neither," said Mei, bobbing up beside us. Her black hair looked like it was painted on. "I thought I was a good swimmer, but she scared me to death back there."

I looked back at Alex standing on the dock with her whistle between her teeth, ready to blow it if we made a wrong move. "Hey, Alex. Instead of sucking on that whistle, why don't you swallow it instead?" Of course she couldn't hear me, but everyone else could. They all laughed at my joke, so I kept going.

"I think Alex needs a nose ring," I said. "Then she could hang her whistle from it. Wouldn't that be a nice fashion statement?"

"JD, stop!" gasped Lauren, treading water just enough to keep her head up. "I can't swim and laugh at the same time!"

"No, don't stop," Courtney said, blowing water out of her nose. "It'll take our minds off how cold we are."

"These are the five areas we'll be working on this

summer: Marco Polo, belly flops, cannonballs, hand-stands . . ."

"That's only four," Mei pointed out.

"And making Alex so mad she swallows that whistle!"

Just then we heard the whistle blow. "Stop horsing around out there!" Alex called across the lake.

Everyone cracked up, so then I said, "Hey, guys, let's all turn around and neigh at her. C'mon, on the count of three . . ."

I counted to three and then spun around in the water and neighed at Alex on the end of the dock, but we were so far away from her now, there was no way she heard me. No one else did it, but the others sure laughed their heads off.

"This class is going to be fun with you in it," said Claudia, the girl who'd looked bored when Alex was talking and who'd kept checking her watch the whole time.

"Yeah, I was about to leave when she went on and on about how hard it was going to be," put in Shelby, a skinny girl with bangs covering her eyes. "But when you stood up and made a big joke of it, I decided to stick it out."

"I fully expect half of you to drown before the class

ends," I said, making my voice growly like Alex's. "And the rest of you better be willing to dedicate your lives to this class or I'll shoot you at sunrise."

"That's just how she talks!" Mei laughed.

"Somebody better tell her this is *summer* camp, not prison camp," I yelled. It was so much fun to laugh at Alex while we were on the other side of the lake. She couldn't reach us out here.

"You should tell her that," Lauren suggested. "It would be so funny if you got out of the water and said that to her!"

"Yeah! Do it!" everybody else was telling me.

"Maybe I will," I said.

"No, don't, JD. You've made her mad enough for one day," warned Courtney. "She'll kick you out, and we all want you in here with us or we'll never make it."

"Okay, fine. I'll try to be good, but it won't be easy." I put my face down and swam faster because I didn't want the rest of them to see my big, goofy smile.

It was working! Boring Judith Duckworth had disappeared, and I was JD, the funniest girl in the class now. But what if I ran out of jokes? I just hoped I could keep up this act forever. Or at least till camp was over.

CHAPTER 5

Friday, June 20

"See, isn't this better than going to activities?" asked Courtney.

"Definitely," I said, trying not to flinch. She pushed my cuticles back with this little tool that looked like a shovel for a Barbie doll.

"How'd you learn to do this?" My other hand soaked in a little pan of warm water. We were sitting on Courtney's bottom bunk, and she had all these instruments lined up on a towel. It looked like she was about to perform surgery on me.

"Just from watching people do them and getting them myself. Haven't you ever had a manicure?" she asked.

"Nope. This is my first." And probably my last. It was

a lot more painful than I thought it was going to be. "Now what are you doing?" She picked up a tiny pair of scissors and grabbed my fingertips.

"Hold still. I have to trim your cuticles. Then we're ready for polish." She looked up at me. "When we're done with your nails, I'll pluck your eyebrows for you."

"Oh, fun! Then you can pull out my toenails with a pair of pliers. I'm *glad* we didn't go to tennis."

Courtney laughed. "Thanks for cabin-sitting with me. You aren't worried we'll get caught, are you?" We were supposed to be at activities right now.

"I never worry about breaking rules. Rules were made to be broken," I bragged.

"That's what I like about you, JD. You're such a rebel."

When Courtney said we should cabin-sit for the afternoon, she tried to talk Mei and Lauren into hanging out with us, but they *were* worried about getting caught, so they went to riflery. Part of me wanted to go with them, because I hadn't been there yet. There were so many cool activities I hadn't tried yet, like rappelling and kayaking, and I'd only been to tennis once. What did it say about me that I'd rather shoot a gun than get a manicure? That I wasn't very good at being a girl. That was something I needed to work on.

"Besides, it's not like they'd punish us if they did catch us," Courtney went on. "They'd just send us to an activity." She buffed my nails with a big pink buffer.

"Exactly. People are always so afraid of getting in trouble. We're brainwashed to follow the rules from the time we're in preschool." I hoped that if anyone did catch us, it would be Alex. I liked Michelle, and I didn't want to be a troublemaker for her. Alex was a different story.

"Do you get in trouble a lot at school?" asked Courtney.

"Oh, yeah. I'm always causing trouble wherever I go," I said, trying not to blush. If only she knew.

"I wish I could be more like you."

"That's ridiculous! Just be yourself," I blurted out. Easy for me to say.

"I wrote some of my friends and my boyfriend Andrew about you. About how you're the life of the Guard Start class and how your jokes get us all through it."

"That's cool." I couldn't believe all the nice things she was saying. I watched her stroke on the red polish she'd picked out. It was a little extreme for me. For Judith. But I figured JD liked extreme colors.

"So do you have a big group of friends you hang out with back home, too?" she asked. It surprised me that she said "too." I had met a lot of people at camp, but I didn't really think of myself as having a big group of friends.

"Yeah, I guess. There's Chloe, Nick, Haley, Jordan, Seth, and Jenna," I said, naming all the popular kids in my school. "We go to the mall and hang out at the food court," I lied. They went to the mall. I once saw them there when I was shopping for new shoes with my grandma.

"Are you going out with any of those guys?" she asked.

"Well, Seth and I were going out, but we broke up. He was way too clingy—texting me about thirty times a day. I couldn't breathe from all that attention." That was exactly what I'd overheard Justin's girlfriend Sarah say about her old boyfriend. Who knew that line would come in handy sometime? "So now Nick and I are going out. He gives me my space."

You're lying. You don't have a boyfriend. You're not popular. And your real name is Judith. Quit putting on this act.

I kept waiting for Courtney to say that, but she just nodded. Every day I expected someone to walk up to me and say, "You're not fooling any of us."

But I was. Apparently. No matter what huge lie I told people, they all seemed to believe me. Why was I even doing this? Courtney already liked me. I didn't have to exaggerate for her.

"That's how Andrew is too," Courtney was saying. "We go out—but in a group. So there's no pressure. He's only sent me one e-mail this whole week. Which is fine with me, because if he was writing me every day, it'd be too much. You know?"

"Exactly," I said. Courtney blew on my nails to dry them. I had to admit, the polish made them look so much better. "Nick hasn't even written me yet, but then I haven't written him, either."

Nick D'Angelo was the cutest guy in my class—dark curly hair, dark brown eyes, and this devilish grin that made him look like he was always up to something. Drool. In my dreams I was getting mail from Nick D'Angelo.

Mail came every day after lunch, and Eda, the camp director, would print out e-mails and stick them in these little wooden boxes on the dining hall porch. Courtney got a stack of e-mails every day from her friends. I'd gotten several e-mails too, but mostly from my family and only a couple from friends. *Girl*friends.

Mom, Dad, and Adam had all sent me e-mails, but Justin hadn't. Mom and Dad both wrote, *Justin sends his love*, and Adam wrote, *Justin told me to say hi*, but I wondered if he really did. I had no idea how he was doing and what was going on back there, because none of them would tell me. They all made it sound like life was great. I knew that wasn't true.

Letting Courtney pluck my eyebrows made my eyes water, but it took my mind off Justin and my family. I felt bad that I could forget about them so easily. All week I'd been having so much fun, I'd barely thought about them. I knew that was one reason my parents had sent me to camp—to give me a break from all the stuff our family was going through. But I still worried about them. I couldn't help it.

"Now let's get some ideas for hairstyles," said Courtney, grabbing a stack of magazines from her trunk for us to look through. "I've been thinking about cutting my hair. Do you think I should?" She pulled her mass of wavy hair together on the back of her neck to give me an idea of what it would look like short.

"You've got great hair," I told her. "You should keep it long."

She sighed. "Maybe so. If I cut it, it would be curlier than ever."

We flipped through the pages of those magazines for probably an hour, with Courtney stopping on almost every page to comment on makeup and clothes and hair that she liked. It was the most boring hour of my life, but I tried to act interested. I really needed to get better at all this girl stuff. What was wrong with me? Why didn't I find this stuff interesting?

"Oh, I love that look," said Courtney, pointing to a model in a black miniskirt with lace leggings.

"You'd look good in that," I told her. I'd look like a gorilla if I tried to dress like that, but Courtney was so petite, she could pull it off. She was probably a size one or zero. Maybe she was even a size minus one, if there was such a thing.

I was a size nine in juniors, and my shoe size was eight and a half. Mom told me she thought my feet wouldn't grow any more, but what if they did? What if I ended up with a size thirteen? Did they even make women's shoes that big?

Courtney sat up and looked out the screen windows. "Omigosh, JD! Look!"

CHAPTER 6

The sky had turned dark gray, and the cabin was all shadowy and dim. We ran to the screen door and looked outside. Rain started pelting down in buckets. Streams of water poured off the roof, and pretty soon a little river had formed in front of the cabin.

"Now I'm really glad we didn't go to activities!" I yelled over the sound of the rain pounding against the cabin roof. Since the cabin had so many screens, it was almost like being outside in the rain—we could smell the wetness and feel it in the air, but with the roof over our heads, we were nice and dry.

Then we saw people running down Middler Line, trying to get to the cabins. One dark figure came crashing through our door as we jumped out of the way.

It was Amber, and she looked like she'd been dunked in the lake. Her hair hung in wet strands like black vines, and her riding boots were covered in mud. She took riding lessons three times a week, and it seemed like she was always wearing those boots.

"It's pouring!" she shouted.

"We noticed!"

Mei and Lauren were the next to show up, both of them completely waterlogged; then Isabel came running in, her eyes wide and her bare legs splashed with mud. Everyone changed out of their wet clothes. I put on my blue hoodie, and Courtney wrapped up in a fuzzy yellow sweater. The whole cabin felt ten degrees cooler from the rain.

Lauren rubbed her blond hair with a towel. "I'm so glad this camp has cabins! Last summer I went to dance camp, and we slept in tents. It rained for three straight days and everything we had got soaked."

Pretty soon everyone came over to Side A, and we all sat around on Courtney's and Amber's bottom bunks.

Mei saw Courtney's magazines and picked one up. "I know—let's play a guessing game. I'll hold up a picture of a model and you guys guess 'real' or 'not real.'"

Everyone laughed. Amber covered her face with her hands. "Don't show me any of those pictures! Whenever I

❤ 52 ❤

look at models, I want to run out and get plastic surgery."

"Oh, Amber! How can you say that?" asked Courtney, hugging her stuffed monkey.

"Uh, hello? Have you seen my nose?" Amber looked around at all of us. "Look, you guys. I know I've got a funny-looking schnoz. You don't have to pretend it's not there." Now I felt awful that I'd always thought of Amber as the flat-nosed girl.

Mei tossed the magazine away in disgust. "You do not need plastic surgery! We should burn these. All they do is make perfectly normal people feel bad about themselves."

"Don't blame it on the magazines. Anyway, all I need to do is look in a mirror to see what's wrong with my face," Courtney said.

"You?" I exclaimed. "You have a cute face, gorgeous hair, and a tiny body. You're perfect from head to toe!" It came out sounding kind of mad, but I'd meant it as a compliment.

"I am not! I hate my cheeks!" Courtney snapped at me. I couldn't tell if she was mad about the "perfect" remark.

I looked at her face and then at her backside. "Which pair of cheeks don't you like?" Everyone burst out laughing, but I wasn't trying to be funny. There was nothing wrong with either set of her cheeks, from what I could tell.

Courtney slapped her face with both hands. "I hate how fat and round my face looks. I wish there were exercises to make my face lose weight."

"You do not have a fat face," we all yelled at her, but she sucked in her cheeks to try to make her face look thin.

"Everyone has something they don't like about themselves," said Lauren. "I can't stand the way my voice sounds."

"What's wrong with your voice?" asked Amber.

"It always sounds hoarse, and I have to clear my throat all the time, and sometimes it comes out sounding squeaky."

Amber sniffed the air. "You guys—do I smell like the barn? I just came from my riding lesson. I love horses, but I'm always afraid they make me smell."

We all told her she smelled fine. I couldn't believe all the weird things people thought were wrong with them. Maybe they were all just making something up—saying they didn't like stuff about themselves so they wouldn't seem conceited. I'd always assumed most girls felt okay about themselves. I thought I was the only one who was so aware of all my flaws.

"When I was about four, I wanted Caucasian eyes," said Mei. "I didn't like that my eyes looked so different from my parents' eyes. Now I'm fine with my eyes, but I hate my ears."

"Why? What's wrong with your ears?" I asked.

"They stick out."

"They do not!" Courtney said.

"Yeah, they do. That's why I always wear my hair down. To cover them up."

Katherine came banging through the door and glanced at all of us hanging out on Side A. Then she went to her side of the cabin without speaking to anyone.

"Uh, Katherine, want to join us?" called Amber, who never wanted anyone to feel left out.

"NO!" she bellowed from across the cabin. We all looked at each other and smiled. We didn't exactly feel deprived of her company.

Isabel and I were the only ones who hadn't said anything yet. If I had to list all the things I didn't like about myself, it would take all week. I didn't like being the size of a linebacker around all these girls who were so petite that a strong breeze would blow them away. I'd recently been reminded of how bushy my eyebrows were and how disgusting my fingernails looked most of the time. Plus my entire wardrobe looked like I was stuck in PE class, 24/7. All I ever wore were basketball shorts and T-shirts in assorted colors. It would take me a lot less time to tell what I *did* like about myself.

But what I hated most about myself was the one thing I couldn't mention—my boring personality. What if right now I told everyone that all week long I'd been putting on an act? It would be the perfect time to do it.

"I hate all my freckles," said Isabel softly. "And of course I'm not good at anything. And I'm short."

"Well, I hate being tall!" I declared, jumping off Courtney's bottom bunk. I banged my head against the springs of my top bunk, and everyone burst out laughing. That was the second time I'd been funny without trying to be. I pulled my blanket off my bunk and wrapped it around my head like a shawl.

"The only thing I could model would be next year's tents. I have a great career ahead of me as a plus-size model." I strutted around between the bunks with the blanket over my head, like I was on the runway. "The paparazzi will tell me to say 'Moo' before they take *my* picture!"

Everyone was laughing but Courtney. "JD, you are not fat!" she insisted.

True, I wasn't fat. Mom always called Justin and Adam her "big, strapping boys." She never called me strapping, but that's what I was. We all had the same genes.

"No, I'm not fat. I'm strapping! I could play tackle football just like my brothers, and I wouldn't even need shoulder pads." It was a little embarrassing to admit how much I hated my size, but at least I was getting noticed. Judith would've sat beside Isabel like a lump and never would've said a word. At least as JD, I got laughs.

The door banged open and Michelle and Meredith walked in. "Hey. What are you guys up to?" Michelle asked.

"Has it stopped raining?" asked Lauren, because they looked pretty dry.

"Yep. Finally," Meredith said. "We were stuck in Senior Lodge. We just saw an awesome mud fight."

Michelle looked at me with the blanket around my head. "Are you cold?"

"We were naming all the things we don't like about ourselves," explained Amber.

"My thighs," said Michelle, without missing a beat. Then she frowned at all of us. "Wait a second. What kind of conversation is this?"

"Well, Lauren thinks I'm a cow, and Mei thinks Courtney's ears are too Caucasian. Isabel said Amber's breath smelled like a horse, and Amber said we all needed plastic surgery." I was pointing fingers at everyone and talking really fast. I hoped everyone would laugh. Luckily, they did. Courtney hit me with her pillow.

Michelle plopped down on her bunk and folded her legs up. Meredith sat on the end of her bed. "Oh, if only you cuties could see yourselves the way I see you! Instead of dissing each other . . ."

"We weren't! We were dissing ourselves," Amber corrected.

Michelle nodded. "Whatever. Instead of dissing anyone, let's all go around and tell each person what we like most about her."

Lauren fell backward on the bunk. "That's corny. Let's not."

"No, we should! I think it's a great idea," said Amber.

"Me too," I said. "I'll start with Amber." I turned to face her. "You are so sweet, and I can tell you're a great person to have as a friend." I felt bad for thinking that Amber would've been a good friend for boring Judith, but JD should hang with Courtney instead. Now the two of us were always together with Lauren and Mei. I wondered if Amber felt left out. "Plus, I think your nose looks mahvelous," I added, because I felt the pressure to keep it funny.

Then everyone else said nice things about Amber. She was an easy one to do. She always had a good attitude about everything. She just went to her riding lessons and wrote poetry during rest hour. Then we picked Courtney, and everyone mostly complimented her on her looks, obviously, but I told her I liked how she was always saying nice things to other people. "And your cheeks look mahvelous," I assured her.

What I wanted to do was hug Courtney and thank her for picking me, Judith Duckworth, to be her friend. Before camp, I never would've thought I could have a bff like Courtney. Sometimes I wondered why she liked me, but then I'd remember. She liked JD. She didn't even know Judith.

Michelle said she liked Mei for her spunk, and I said I liked how she always did the right thing. What I meant was, I thought it was great how she always stood up for Isabel when Katherine was mean to her, but of course I couldn't say it that way.

"You're really good at keeping the peace," said Mei to Meredith, even though she'd missed most of the conversation.

Meredith had a funny way of putting her hands on her hips and saying, "This is not a crisis" any time anyone got upset or mad. Mei was good at sticking up for Isabel against Katherine, but Meredith kept things from getting out of hand in the first place.

Lauren got embarrassed when it was her turn. People mentioned her oh-so-blond hair and limber dancer's body. Amber grinned at me and said, "I think Lauren's voice sounds mahvelous."

"Oh, snap! Now what do I say?" I wailed. "Lauren, out of the whole Guard Start class, you try harder than anyone." She rolled her eyes and looked out the window. "I mean, I like how dedicated you are to the class. I could learn something from you." This morning Lauren had been the last one to finish her laps. She'd gotten mad at us all for clapping when she finally made it to the end of the dock.

When it was Isabel's turn, everyone said nice things about her personality, which made me mad. Did they have to be so obvious? Courtney had gotten so many compliments about her looks, and now they were going on and on about Isabel's personality. Why didn't they just put a bag over her head? "Isabel, you have beautiful eyes and a great smile," I said. She looked at me and grinned.

"I have a lot of respect for Isabel. She really has a desire to succeed," said Michelle, smiling. We all admired the way Isabel worked so hard at learning to swim.

"Now it's your turn," Amber said, pointing at me.

"You are the funniest person I've ever met in my entire life." Everyone else agreed, so I felt like a million bucks.

Little did they know I wasn't really funny, at least not naturally funny. All week I'd worried about running out of jokes. How long could I keep this up? Every single time there was a pause in the conversation, I'd think, "Say something funny now," and I was always afraid I'd draw a blank.

"You have a great personality," said Isabel, so softly I could barely hear her.

"Thanks!" But should I take credit for a good personality that wasn't even mine? I'd given up trying to act like Chloe; I couldn't do it. JD was a lot louder and more obnoxious than Chloe and not so quick and clever with the comebacks. But my new personality was warmer and fuzzier than Chloe's, more like a big teddy bear. Chloe had a way of cutting people down to get laughs. It seemed like I mostly made fun of myself.

"And you're a great athlete. So stop calling yourself a linebacker. I wish I had half your strength and endurance," said Lauren, looking at her fingernails the whole time.

Michelle grinned at me. "What I like most about JD is her sensitivity."

I had no idea what that meant, but I liked the way it sounded.

Camp was so much fun. It was hard to believe we'd only been together for a week. It seemed longer. Being around a bunch of girls was a lot different from my life back home with a house full of boys. Maybe this was what it felt like to have sisters.

Saturday, June 21

"I have absolutely nothing to wear tonight," I said, looking at the pile of clothes I'd pulled out of my trunk. It was such a girl thing to say, but it was true. Luckily, my brothers weren't around to hear me or they'd never stop teasing me.

"Maybe you can borrow something of mine," offered Amber. She'd just come back from the showers, and she was still wrapped up in a towel.

"Are you a size nine?" I asked.

"Uh, I wear mostly five." She shrugged and smiled at me hopefully.

"Thanks anyway," I told her.

"I'm glad we did our nails yesterday," said Courtney. "One less thing to worry about today."

We were one hour away from having a dance with the boys from Camp Crockett. Everyone in the cabin was rushing around getting ready.

"Should I wear my hair down?" asked Lauren as she brushed her hair in front of the little mirror on the wall. All week I'd never seen her without her blond ponytail.

"I think you should," Courtney said, squeezing next to her to look in the mirror while she put on some mascara. "And I can't wait to see you dance tonight."

"Oh, please. I bet none of those guys can move at all," snorted Lauren. She had shown us some dance moves this morning when we first heard there might be a dance tonight. She was an awesome dancer. "I've been taking lessons since I was four," she'd told us with a little smile.

"Well, I'm ready," Mei announced, coming over to Side A. She had on a pink skirt and a white shirt, and she looked adorable. "Think these guys will actually dance with us?" she asked, trying out some of the steps Lauren had shown us. "Or will they stand around and ignore us?"

"They'll ignore us. They're all jerks," we heard Katherine say from Side B.

"Way to look on the bright side, Katherine," said Mei over her shoulder.

"I always get nervous before dances. I'm not good at talking to boys," Amber admitted.

I slammed my trunk shut. "Why would you be nervous talking to boys? Boys are . . ." I tried to think of the right words. "Boys are like dogs. They're smelly and playful and they scratch themselves a lot."

"Omigosh, JD!" gasped Amber. "You always crack me up. 'Boys Are Like Dogs.' That would make a great title." She grabbed a spiral notebook from beside her bed and jotted something down. Maybe I'd given her inspiration for a new poem.

"So you're saying you don't get nervous around boys?" asked Courtney, looking at me skeptically.

"No, I don't. Remember, I have two brothers, and their friends are always hanging around our house at all hours of the day. I know how to talk to boys," I said. Justin and Adam had two friends I was totally in love with—Ben and Ryan. They thought of me as just a little sister, so I could tease them and punch them in the arm and pull their hair. I never got nervous around those guys.

Lauren turned away from the mirror. "So, you want to give us any advice?"

"Just watch a pro in action tonight," I bragged. "I'll have a boyfriend before the night is over."

"Oh, really?" said Mei.

"Okay, JD. If you say so," Lauren said.

Obviously they didn't believe me, and I couldn't really blame them. What was I saying? But now I had to follow through.

"What about Nick?" asked Courtney.

I came so close to asking "Nick who?" until I remembered that in my fantasy world I was going out with Nick D'Angelo. "Well, what Nick doesn't know won't hurt him, will it?" I said.

Michelle and Alex came in and asked us why we were all dressed up. "Do you guys know something we don't know?" asked Michelle with a sly grin.

No one had said for sure yet that we were having a dance. They worried that if they made it definite, we'd all be so excited we wouldn't go to any activities all day, so they kept us in suspense until the last moment. At least if there wasn't a dance I'd be off the hook for finding a boyfriend.

"We were tired of looking like slobs all week," said Courtney, batting her eyelashes at Michelle.

"I seriously have nothing to wear!" I yelled.

"Want to borrow something of mine?" asked Michelle, saving my life.

"Oh, you mean there *is* a dance tonight?" Lauren said.

Michelle looked at me and smiled. "I never said that! JD can borrow my clothes anytime."

We looked through her clothes until we'd picked out a pair of chocolate-colored cargos and a tan tank. I rolled the pants legs up so they didn't look too short. "Then layer this on the top." She handed me a short-sleeved shirt with a tiny flower print. "Leave this shirt unbuttoned. What do you think, everyone?" She spun me around for inspection.

"You look great, JD!" said Amber.

"Here, wear these earrings," Lauren offered, bringing me a pair of little gold hoops. "And I've got a necklace for you too." She squinted while she put her earrings in for me.

"When you're done with her, bring her to me so I can do her hair and makeup," said Courtney, putting on lip gloss in front of the mirror.

"Oh, thank God I've got an entire pit crew to dress me! I could never do this on my own!" They all laughed, but it was true.

While Courtney styled my hair and did my makeup, everyone else stood around and watched. When she was finished, she wouldn't let me look in the little mirror. "Let's go to Solitary, where you can really get a good look."

We all trooped down Middler Line to the bathrooms. Courtney grabbed my arm as we went through the doorway. "Close your eyes." She led me over to the full-length mirror next to the row of sinks and stopped. "Okay, open."

I opened my eyes and looked in the mirror at someone who looked like a really good version of me. "Wow!" I said. Lauren, Amber, and Mei stood behind me, grinning. "Thanks, guys! I couldn't have done it without you. And I seriously mean that."

Solitary was packed with other girls using the sinks and pushing for a turn in front of the mirror, so we left for the dining hall, since it was time for dinner anyway.

"Garlic bread, anyone?" asked Michelle with a grin, passing the plate around our table. I took two pieces, but Courtney frowned at me.

"You think that's a good idea right before a dance?" she asked.

"What? Too many carbs?" I wondered.

"No, goofy. Garlic. If you want to gargle half a bottle of mouthwash, go ahead."

In the middle of dinner the CATs (Counselor Assistants in Training) came in clapping and singing. I loved the CATs; it was their job to make sure all the campers were having a good time. They were sixteen, so they were kind of in between campers and counselors. When they announced that we were going to Camp Crockett for a dance, the whole dining hall went crazy.

"But be careful!" the CATs yelled. "If those Crockett boys want you to sneak away to the bushes for a make-out session, we'll be watching to make sure that nobody leaves the dining hall porch!" Then they sang this crazy song, holding flashlights and shining them all over everyone.

> Porch Patrol! Porch Patrol!
> Start yellin' for that good ole Porch Patrol!
> If he tries to make first base, you had better slap his face,
> And start yellin' for that good ole Porch Patrol!

When they'd finished singing and sat down at their table in the middle of the dining hall, Lauren asked, "Are they really going to the dance dressed like that?" They were all wearing camouflage T-shirts and pants, and they had leaves and little tree branches stuck in their hair and taped to their clothes.

"They sure are," said Alex. "So don't let them catch you."

"You mean they'll be watching us? Has anyone ever gotten caught?" I asked.

"Of course not," said Katherine. "They sing that same stupid song every year. Who would want to be seen with any of those Crockett creeps?"

"The point is, while you're at Camp Crockett you're not to leave their dining hall. And if anyone does try to leave, the Porch Patrol will stop you. So I expect you all to act like young ladies this evening!" warned Michelle.

So nobody had ever been caught by the Porch Patrol. Wouldn't *that* be a great way to make a name for myself? Maybe no one had ever been caught because no one had ever tried to sneak away.

But wasn't there a first time for everything?

CHAPTER 8

When we walked into Camp Crockett's dining hall, I saw Natasha hanging out with her new bff, Ashlin. I ran over and gave her a hug like I always did whenever I saw her. It was sort of sad that Natasha and I had different sets of friends now.

Lauren, Mei, Courtney, and I were all standing together. All the boys were across from us, and so far no one was dancing, even though the music was playing.

I decided I needed to work fast. I couldn't stand around waiting for some guy to find me. I had to go to him. Most girls were hoping to dance with some cute guys and maybe even meet someone they really liked. That didn't matter to me. I just needed to make it look like I'd found a guy who liked me.

I looked at the crowd of boys. There sure were a lot of shrimpy guys who went to this camp. I wanted to find someone who wasn't a foot shorter than I was, and judging by the looks of this crowd, that wasn't going to be easy.

The guys stood around talking to each other. Every now and then one of them would look over in our direction, like they were checking to see if we were still there.

"See anyone you like?" asked Courtney.

"Maybe. How about you?" I said.

"Yeah. See the guy in the green Hurley shirt? He keeps looking over here."

"Hey, you in the green shirt. Come over and dance with my friend," I said, kind of loud, but not loud enough for him to actually hear me.

"JD, stop!" hissed Courtney. "Try not to embarrass all of us, please!"

"Oh, don't worry. I won't embarrass anyone but myself. Why don't you all just watch and see how it's done?"

I walked straight over to where three guys were standing. Two of them were close to my height. When they saw me coming toward them, they all got panicked looks on their faces, like they didn't know what I was going to do to them. Most girls didn't realize that boys were scared of us half the time.

"Hey, guys. Wassup?"

"Hi," one of them answered. The other two just stood there.

"My friends dared me to come talk to you guys. They didn't think I'd do it, so help me out here, okay?"

"Sure," said the talker of the group.

"I'm JD, by the way."

"Oh. I'm Lance." He was around my height, and he wore glasses and had a really severe case of bed head.

"I'm David," said the other tall guy. He had braces and a buzz cut, and his face was beefy and round.

"I'm Michael," said the short guy. He wasn't really that short, just not as tall as the rest of us.

"What's JD short for?" asked Lance.

"Jamaica Daytona," I said, looking at him with a straight face.

"What a weird name. No wonder you go by your initials," Michael said.

"Well, my parents love the beach. Good thing they're not into mountains or I might've been named Everest Rushmore." It was a lot of fun telling crazy stories to people. Amazingly, they always believed me, or at least they hardly ever questioned me.

The guys looked at me like they didn't know what to do next. I glanced over to where my friends were, and they were all watching me. When Courtney saw me, she raised her eyebrows. I had to make this look good. Time to bring up the one subject that every boy in the world was interested in.

"Wow. This dance pretty much sucks, doesn't it?" I asked them.

"Yeah," they all said at the same time.

"You know what would make this a really good dance? If we had a room with a long row of TVs and about five or six different game systems," I said.

"Oh, sweet!" groaned Lance, like he could picture a setup like that.

Michael and David nodded. "That would be awesome."

"So which systems do you guys have?" I asked.

Then all three of them were talking at the same time. Wii, PS2 and 3, DS, PSP, Xbox 360—they rattled them all off. I stood in the middle and let them talk. I glanced across the dining hall and saw Mei's jaw drop.

"Yeah, have you ever played Twilight Princess on Wii?" I asked Lance. He was the one I liked best. Behind his glasses, I noticed he had beautiful gray eyes, and when he smiled, he had a dimple in the side of his cheek.

"Oh! I don't have it, but my friend Gabe does. It's pretty tight."

"I've got it for GameCube," said Michael. "My favorite part is when you're battling the monkeys."

"On Madden, do you guys ever set a player's weight as high as it'll go and his speed at zero so he can barely move?" I asked.

Lance let out a loud cackle. "I love doing that! One time I made this one player really weak. He tried to catch a pass, but he fell over and couldn't get up!"

The four of us spent at least ten minutes talking about all our favorite games and what levels we'd gotten to on all of them. Then I said, "Hang on a second, guys. I need to talk to my friends, but I'll be right back."

I walked across the dining hall to my crew. "Wipe that smirk off your face!" said Lauren when I walked up to her.

Mei grabbed me by both arms. "How? How? Just tell us how you did that!"

"What were you guys talking about, JD?" asked Courtney. "You sure had their attention."

I shrugged. "Nothing, really. Just guy stuff. Look, I gotta go. My boys are waiting for me. Do any of you want to dance with one of them?"

"I'll take the cute one," Courtney said.

"The one with the dark hair? That's Michael. I'll see what I can do." It didn't surprise me that Courtney would pick Michael. He was the cutest of the three, but I still preferred Lance's gray eyes. Plus he was taller than Michael.

Then I walked back over to the guys. "Look, guys, I know it would be a lot more fun to stand around and talk about video games all night, but my friends are bored. So why don't you come over and meet them? You don't have to dance or anything."

I walked off like I assumed they would follow me, and they did. I'd never been the one who's always telling other people what to do, but the weird thing was, it worked. At least most of the time. It seemed like most people spent a lot of time waiting for someone to tell them what to do. I figured I might as well be the one who did the telling.

While my friends were introducing themselves to the guys, I decided it was time to put my plan in action. I leaned over to Lance and said, "I don't like to dance, do you?"

"No, I suck at it," he answered. He had really long legs, and he moved like he wasn't used to walking on them yet.

"Hey, want to go out on the porch? It's pretty stuffy in here."

Lance shrugged. "Okay, sure."

He followed me outside to the porch, where a bunch of people were hanging out and talking. Some people were sitting on the rails and others were just standing around. It was almost dark. Crickets were chirping, and a few moths fluttered around the porch lights.

"So, do you know any good cheat codes for the Sims?" I asked.

"Yeah, freeall, fisheye, midas. You enter them by holding L1, L2, R1, R2."

While Lance chattered away about the Sims, I glanced around. Besides a bunch of campers, a few Crockett and Pine Haven counselors were out here too, but I didn't see any of the CATs. Did that mean they weren't really on Porch Patrol? Had the whole thing been a joke? If we walked away from the dining hall right now, would anybody notice us?

"It's a pretty nice night out, isn't it?" I said. "Feel like taking a walk? I've never been to Camp Crockett before. You could show me around."

My heart started pounding a little when I said that. Getting caught *sounded* like a great idea when I'd first thought of it, but now that it was time to actually go through with it, I wasn't so sure.

Lance scratched his ear. "Uh, I don't think we can

leave. The counselors told us to stay around the dining hall for the whole dance." His feet kicked against the porch rails.

"Really? That's weird. I wonder why they'd even care. Have you ever played Destroy All Humans?" I asked. Think, think, think. What excuse could I make for us to leave the dining hall?

Lance went off on what a great game that was. I noticed there were steps at either end of the porch. The ones we were closest to were by the parking area, and there were lights shining on all the Pine Haven vans and trucks we'd come over in. At the far end of the porch, though, there weren't any lights. And there weren't very many people hanging out there either. If we did try to leave, that should definitely be our exit.

"It's sure crowded out here. Let's move down there where there aren't as many people." I headed for the far end of the porch and Lance followed, telling me about the time he leveled out all of Rockwell's buildings. So far we hadn't broken any rules, but my heart wouldn't stop pounding. It was easy for me to talk about what a rule breaker I was to everyone. Now it was time to really prove it. But how could I convince Lance to go along with me?

Maybe I should tell him I needed to make a phone call. I had a poor sick grandma in the hospital who might not make it through the night. Couldn't he help me find a phone somewhere?

"I have this old copy of *Tips and Tricks*. It has a strategy guide that helped me get through all the levels of that game," said Lance.

"Really? I would *love* to see those. Do you remember any of them?" I asked. How exactly does one get from the subject of aliens conquering Earth to a poor sick grandma? *My poor grandma used to love watching me use my disintegrator ray to reduce my enemies to dust. But she's really sick now, and . . .*

"Well, it's in my cabin. I brought a stack of *Tips and Tricks* with me in case—"

"It's in your cabin?" I said. "Can I see it? Please, oh please? I've been stuck on level eighteen forever. I've gotta see that guide!" Okay, now this just might work. I felt a little braver now. I reminded myself that JD didn't get nervous when it came to getting into trouble.

"Uh, I don't think we're supposed to—"

"Oh Lance, don't tell me you're one of those nerdy guys who's always worried about following all the rules. I know you're not like *that*." I was down the steps before he could get another word out. "Which way is your cabin? We can be there and back in ten minutes. Nobody will ever know we're gone."

I walked fast, going in the opposite direction of where all the counselors were at the other end of the porch. It was pretty dark now, and I hoped we wouldn't get all the way to Lance's cabin before *somebody* saw us. It would be okay to get into a little trouble, but I didn't want to cause a huge uproar. Lance trotted to catch up with me.

"No, really. I think we should—"

"Is this the way?" I pointed down a dirt path that looked like it might lead to some cabins.

"No, that goes to the Mites cabins. I'm a Newt. Our cabins are that way, but—"

"This way? I'm so glad you brought those magazines with you. Looking at strategy guides will be so much better than being stuck at this dance." I couldn't really see his face in the dark, but he was at least keeping up with me now. The grass was all dewy and wet, and the crickets were singing like crazy.

"Uh, JD—I'm not sure we can—"

"C'mon. Don't be so nervous!" My gosh, were all boys this shy? If they got this stressed over showing a girl their strategy guides, how did they ever get up the nerve to kiss someone?

"Hey! Where are you guys going?"

Finally! We turned around, and the beam of a flashlight bounced across our faces. All I could see were two dark forms standing there, shining a light in our eyes.

Perfect. The Porch Patrol really was on duty after all.

CHAPTER 9

I recognized them when they got a little closer: Madison Abernathy and Lydia Duncan. They were still dressed in camouflage.

"What are you two doing?" asked Madison. She was really pretty, with long dark hair. She had a few leafy twigs sticking out all over the place.

"Uh, we . . . uh," stuttered Lance. His mouth hung open, and the light reflected off the lenses of his glasses. Now I felt bad for getting him into trouble.

"We were just going for a walk," I said. "Lance was showing me the Camp Crockett sights." I gave them both a big smile. No way could I tell them we were on our way to his cabin.

"No, you're not," said Lydia. "You guys know you're

not supposed to leave the dining hall. Get back to the dance."

"Are we in big trouble? Please don't tell Eda," I begged. Actually, I didn't care if she told Eda or not. The more people who knew about it, the better.

"Just get going." Madison shone her flashlight at us one more time, so I couldn't see their expressions. Did they think it was funny they'd caught us? Or were they mad? Their voices had been all stern-sounding. When we walked past them, I wanted to grab Lance's hand so it would look like we were up to *something*, but I didn't want to make the poor guy faint.

"Uh," said Lance. He was still speechless.

"Hey, it's okay. They won't do anything to us," I whispered to him. Madison and Lydia walked behind us, like they didn't trust us to find the dining hall on our own.

When we got back to the porch, it seemed like there were about twenty or thirty people watching us as we walked up. I bumped against Lance a couple of times to make it look like we were a real couple who'd been caught making out in the dark. He scooted over each time I did it, though, so I stopped.

Maybe I should've smeared my lip gloss before everybody saw us. Why didn't I think of that before? Chloe Carlson would've thought of that. Wait a second, Chloe

Carlson wouldn't need to smear her own lip gloss; the boy she was with would've done it for her. But so what? Chloe wasn't the one who got caught this time. *I* was. And things couldn't have been more perfect. It was exactly like I thought it would be.

"Lance! You da man!" a boy yelled from the porch. Somebody whistled as we walked up the steps. I had a little smile on my face as everyone watched us. Lance stared at his shoelaces the whole time.

When we walked into the dining hall, a Camp Crockett counselor gave us a long, intense look; then he walked toward us. I was afraid he was Lance's counselor, and now he was going to yell at us for leaving the dining hall. But for some reason, he was looking right at me. He didn't even notice Lance was there.

"Hey, don't I know you?" he asked.

The second he said that, I recognized him. Brandon Matheson, a guy who used to play football at Central. A teammate of Justin's!

What was *he* doing here? I did not want to be recognized by anyone from home! Especially not in front of Lance. If Lance hadn't been with me, I would've taken off running in the opposite direction.

Brandon pointed at me. "I got it! You're a Duckworth, aren't you? Yeah! I remember you from all the practices!"

"Oh, hi," I said. *Now, bye. See ya later. Adios, amigo.* "You're Brandon, right?" I asked him through my clenched smile. His hair was longer than it used to be, and he looked a little older.

"Yeah, that's right. So you're going to Pine Haven, huh?" asked Brandon.

"Uh, yeah." My head bounced up and down like a bobblehead. Maybe we could keep the topic of conversation on camp instead of football. "You're a counselor, I guess. That must be fun. What's your activity?" Lance looked back and forth between me and Brandon. So far he hadn't missed a word of this conversation.

"I'm on the hiking staff. Hey—how's Justin doing?"

"He's doing great! I'll tell him I saw you. Wow! He'll really be surprised. This is Lance, by the way. Brandon's from my hometown." Maybe now we could say our good-byes and walk away. I held my breath and hoped that Brandon wouldn't say anything else about Justin and football in front of Lance.

"Hey, dude. What's up?" Brandon said without even looking at Lance. He was completely focused on me, unfortunately. "Well, I heard what happened. What a shame. I couldn't believe it." He said it in a sorry-your-dog-died kind of voice.

So he *had* heard about what happened. I was hoping

that maybe if he was away at college, he didn't know all the gory details. No such luck.

"Yeah. Well, things are okay," I said, my head bobbing up and down like crazy. "So you're in college now?"

"Yeah, I just finished my first year at Auburn. I'm playing lacrosse now."

"Really? Cool. Lacrosse is a great sport." *In fact, let's talk about lacrosse from now on, and not speak of football ever again.*

"Yeah. I didn't get a football scholarship. I considered trying out as a walk-on, but I'm an engineering major, and I really needed time for my studies. With lacrosse, I can play a sport without it taking up all my time."

I nodded. Obviously, Brandon had been bitten by the chatty bug seconds before he'd run into us.

"Hey, listen. Tell your brother I said hi. Hope everything works out for him. I was real sorry to hear what happened. It hurt the whole team."

"Okay, thanks. I will. Bye, Brandon!" I took two steps back, hoping he wouldn't say anything else before I could finally get away.

But he was done. He walked off.

Oh my God! My heart hammered in my chest. My face felt flaming hot. All I wanted to do was get as far away from Brandon Matheson as I possibly could. I pushed through the crowd of people, not even caring at this point if Lance was still following me or not.

How was it possible that I'd been recognized when I was two hundred miles from home? And that the person who recognized me not only knew Justin, but used to play football with him? What were the odds? Brandon Matheson, of all people! And when did he turn into such a yakker?

"Uh, JD?"

I spun around to see Lance trailing along behind me. "What?" I snapped at him.

Lance drew back like I'd spit in his eye. "What was that all about?"

"Oh, Brandon. He knows my brother. Used to play football with him. Are you as thirsty as I am?" I took off toward the refreshment table at a mad run. Lance tried to keep up with me.

"What was all that stuff about 'I heard what happened'?" asked Lance. Boy, he'd certainly gotten curious all of a sudden.

I stopped at the refreshment table, grabbed a cup of red bug juice, and gulped it down. "Oh, that. Justin got injured. Pulled his quadriceps. He might not be able to play next season."

"Oh." Lance took a drink of bug juice and looked around. "I wonder where Mike and David are."

I let out a sigh and concentrated on getting my pulse down from rapid to normal. My hand holding the paper cup was shaking, so I crumpled it up and tossed it into the trash can.

It wasn't a total lie. Justin had pulled his quadriceps once during his sophomore year, and he missed the last two games of the season. I was so relieved Brandon hadn't blabbed too much about what had happened. Lance didn't need to hear that. No one needed to hear that.

"Is it true?"

I spun around to see Katherine beside me. "I heard you and some guy got caught by the Porch Patrol." She gave Lance a quick look and then sneered at me.

"Yeah. So?" I did not feel like dealing with Katherine right now.

"So what you were doing?" she asked.

"Katherine, if you want the latest news, check the headlines every day." I stomped off through the crowd of dancers. Lance ran up behind me.

"Sorry about that. I didn't know we'd get in trouble," he said.

I slowed down as we weaved in and out of the

people on the dance floor. "It's okay. I don't mind," I told him over my shoulder. Poor guy. He'd put up with a lot tonight. "Anyway, it was my idea to leave the dining hall in the first place, remember?"

We moved over to the edge of the dance floor and sat in some chairs along the wall. "Thanks for hanging out with me tonight. I had a great time," I told him. "Too bad we couldn't have played a few levels of Destroy All Humans."

"Yeah." Lance nodded. He sat with his feet sticking way out, and a couple of people stumbled over them as they walked by. He was tall and goofy, but I still liked the guy. He really was a good sport. "I've never met a girl who knows so much about video games. I didn't even want to come to this dance, but it turned out pretty okay."

By now everyone was slow dancing, and we sat there and watched them. Now I was wishing I hadn't made all those comments about not liking to dance. Lance would be okay to slow dance with. He had beautiful gray eyes and he was fun to hang out with, and he'd followed me all over the place tonight.

Maybe at the next dance. Hey, if I could convince him to leave the dining hall, it couldn't be that hard to figure out how to get him out on the dance floor.

When the dance ended, everyone crowded through the doors to go outside.

"Sorry I got us in trouble," I told Lance. "Maybe I'll see you at the next dance?"

"Sure. See ya later!" He'd found David and Mike, and they were dragging him away, asking a bunch of questions. I wondered if he would tell them what we were really doing. Probably. He didn't seem to have a clue what the Porch Patrol was really there for.

When I walked up to the truck that would take us all back to camp, everyone swarmed around me.

"So you really got caught?" asked Mei. "Was it the guy with the glasses?"

"What were you doing?" Lauren asked.

"JD, you *have* to tell us what happened!" said Courtney.

I plastered a huge grin on my face and said, "I don't kiss and tell!" Then I refused to say another word, even though they kept pumping me for more info.

It would've been a perfect night if it hadn't been for Brandon Matheson. It was bad enough that Lance had witnessed that little meeting. What if one of my friends had been with me when I ran into him? Or Michelle? Almost every day Michelle asked me more questions about Justin and Adam. I wished she'd never even seen those pictures of them playing football. There was no way I could tell her I didn't want to talk about my own brothers.

"Climb in!" yelled Jerry. He was Pine Haven's hiking guide, and he'd driven the white truck we had to ride in. We all piled into the back and sat on the benches that lined the sides and the back of the truck.

"So, are you going to tell me about it?" whispered Courtney.

"I will, but not now," I said. At least Brandon hadn't called me Judith. Maybe he didn't remember my name. I was only Justin's kid sister to him.

The truck rumbled down the road, and everyone laughed when we passed under the Camp Crockett sign, because there was pink underwear hanging all over it. I could pull off being JD at camp, but when camp was over, then what?

There were times when it felt like I'd always been JD. Sometimes I completely forgot about my old life as Judith. Until it would come sneaking up on me, like Brandon Matheson. *Don't I know you?*

No, Brandon, you *don't* know me. And Courtney, Lauren, Mei—they don't know me either. How could they know me?

They don't even know my name.

CHAPTER 10

Monday, June 23

"So how would you rate him, on a scale of one to ten?" asked Mei.

"Oh, I'd say about a seven," I said. I kicked with my feet under water so I wouldn't splash everyone around me.

"A seven? Is that all?" Courtney asked, swimming up beside me. Out of everyone in the class, she was the one who was most able to keep up with me. But when we swam laps, I didn't go fast. It was more fun for all of us to stay in a group and talk.

"Okay, an eight, then," I said. "Wait up for Lauren, you guys." We all slowed down so Lauren could catch up to us.

"Don't let me hold everyone else up!" Lauren snapped

at us when she got closer. We all felt bad that she had such a hard time. She tried her best, but it was always a struggle.

"JD, admit it. Nothing happened between you and that guy," said Claudia. "I bet he didn't lay a hand on you. Or a lip!"

The whole class cracked up over Claudia's lip remark. She obviously saw through me, more than anyone else. I hadn't exactly lied about what happened when Lance and I got caught by the Porch Patrol on Saturday night. Everyone had just assumed we'd been kissing. Of course, saying "I don't kiss and tell" whenever anyone asked me about what happened probably had a little something to do with it.

"Okay, whatever. Believe what you want to believe," I told the others. "Maybe Lance and I weren't kissing when those two CATs caught us. And maybe his breath didn't smell like Skittles."

"Like Skittles? His breath smelled like Skittles?" asked Shelby, pushing her bangs out of her eyes.

"Yeah, but I didn't mind," I said. "He did have a pucker like a fish, though." Now everyone was laughing over my remark. Poor Lance. He really was a nice guy, and I didn't plan on making fun of him. I was just trying to think of something funny to say. Good thing he'd never know I'd said that about him.

"Only JD would be crazy enough to get caught by the Porch Patrol," said Courtney.

"Yeah! I couldn't believe the way you walked over and started talking to all those guys. You definitely have a way with boys, JD," Mei said, paddling beside me.

"What's all the discussion about?" yelled Alex as we swam up close to the dock. "Everyone out on the side. We're going to work on reaching and throwing assists today."

Alex told Claudia to jump in and show signs of distress. Then she demonstrated how to do a reaching assist by lying on our stomachs on the dock and reaching out with an arm, and then holding on to a rung of the ladder and reaching out with a leg. Next she threw a ring buoy out to Claudia and pulled her in.

"Okay, now I want you guys to try it in pairs. Claudia, out of the water. Courtney, you jump in and Claudia will do both a reach and a pull assist with you."

The rest of us sat on the edge of the dock to watch the exercise.

"You guys want to know something?" whispered Mei, hugging her towel around her shoulders. "I've never been kissed. Pathetic, huh?"

"No, it's not!" I said. "Look, it's really no big deal. It's not like I saw fireworks or anything." I dangled my feet over the edge of the dock, my toes touching the water. I watched a few little tadpoles dart up to the dock and then swim away.

"Well, I haven't really been either," Lauren confessed. The sunlight made her squint, so she kept her hand in front of her eyes. "Except for Will Thurmond. He kissed me on the playground when we were in second grade. But I'm not sure that really counts. It was on the cheek."

"Sure it counts," I told her. "If you want it to."

"Ugh!" she groaned. "If Will Thurmond counts as my first kiss, I'm even more pathetic than you are, Mei. He was always having nosebleeds!"

"This guy kissed me at my school's fall festival last year," said Shelby. "We were in the haunted house. I was *so* not expecting it. We'd just stuck our hands in bowls of Jell-O and spaghetti, and then all of a sudden—smack!"

We were all laughing, but I felt sort of bad. It was fun getting so much attention for being caught by the Porch Patrol. That part had gone exactly the way I'd hoped it would. And now my reputation as a rule breaker was really growing. But if my friends were going to get a complex over it, I wasn't sure it was worth it. I didn't want Lauren and Mei to think something was wrong with them because they'd never been kissed.

Because I hadn't either. I hadn't even had a peck on the cheek by a second-grade nosebleeder. Last year I'd been shooting hoops with some boys during recess. I was guarding Jacob Zinner when I noticed that *his* breath smelled like Skittles, and for a second I'd wondered what it would be like to kiss him. *That* was the closest I'd ever come to being kissed. Just thinking about it.

"Good job!" yelled Alex from the water. "Okay, now let's have Mei and Lauren."

Lauren and Mei took a turn while Claudia and Courtney came over and sat down. "What were you guys laughing about?" asked Courtney, dripping all over us.

"Oh, nothing," I said. I wanted to get off the subject of Lance and kissing for a while. Shelby and I scooted over to make room for them to sit down beside us.

"Oh, JD—I almost forgot to tell you. Yesterday during rest hour, Michelle was writing mommy letters," said Courtney, wrapping herself up in her towel.

"So?" I asked. Michelle had asked us all about our favorite activities so she could write the weekly letter home to our parents, telling them how we were doing.

"So—what if she tells your parents you got caught by the Porch Patrol?"

Claudia shook her head. "Nah, she wouldn't do that. Eda doesn't want the counselors to say anything bad about us to our parents, unless there's some real problem." She looked at her watch. "Fifteen more minutes." Claudia was always counting down the minutes till class was over, like she had someplace better to be.

"Anyway, it wouldn't surprise my parents that I'd gotten in trouble," I said. "You know what I always say—rules were made to be broken."

But Courtney had me worried about something. I had to remember to tell Michelle to call me Judith in the letter home to my parents. If she wrote something like *JD is working very hard in her Guard Start class*, they wouldn't know who she was talking about. And I'd have to find a time to tell her when nobody else was around.

Also, mentioning the letter home to my parents made me feel guilty. I'd barely thought about my family for days. I was so completely caught up in my camp life.

It seemed like I had always woken up to the sound of a big bell being rung and the feel of cool mountain air drifting in through the window screens. Every morning we cleaned the cabin, ate breakfast, and went to activities. Then it was lunchtime, rest hour, and more activities. Then dinner, evening program in Middler Lodge, and bed. I loved the pattern of every day. It was like a school schedule, only everything centered around fun instead of work. It seemed like I'd swum in this lake hundreds of times, and I'd sat on this dock and gazed at these mountains my whole life. It was amazing how easy it was to put my family and my old life out of my mind.

Shelby and Courtney cheered for Lauren and Mei while they did the exercise. Lauren splashed water at us. She seemed to think it was a pity remark when we told her she did a good job at something. The truth was, she was really good at doing the service hours and helping out with swim lessons. And she was always the first to finish the workbook exercises we had to do. It was only the swimming part she had trouble with.

"What's up with you? You look so serious all of a sudden," said Courtney, shading her face with her hand while she stared at me.

If I went more than five minutes without cracking a joke, everyone looked at me and asked me what was wrong. It was just what I'd always worried about— that I'd run out of funny things to say and then everyone would find out the truth. There were times when I wanted to yell, "I'm sick of this!" and go back to being Judith.

"Why'd you have to mention the mommy letters?" I asked her. "I miss my mommy." At least now that I'd thought about her for the first time in days, I missed her. "Don't you miss your mommy?"

"Of course," Courtney said.

"I miss my mommy, oh yes, I do, I miss my mommy, and I'll be true!" I started singing to the tune of one of the camp songs. "When she's not with me, I'm blue, I'm blue-hoo," I sang in a really deep voice, "oh, Mommy, I miss you!"

"Keep it down before Alex hears you," Claudia told me.

"Good idea," said Courtney, giving me a look and jerking her head to the side.

"What? Don't you like my singing?" I wailed. "Is there anything wrong with being a loving daughter singing a song to my mother? Huh? You got a problem wit' dat?" I shook my fists at the rest of them. But they were all acting like I'd just cursed my mother's good name or something. Shelby stared out at the lake. Claudia and Courtney both glared at me. For some reason, nobody liked my joke.

"Huh! What's wrong with this crowd?" I went on. "I happen to love my mother. Ouch!" Courtney had poked me in the ribs as hard as she could. "What? You don't love your mother?" I asked her.

"JD, shut up," Claudia warned. "Your joke's not

funny, so drop it. I can't believe Alex hasn't heard you yet." She glanced at her watch again.

"Shelby, don't you miss your mommy?" I asked.

Shelby stared at the lake and didn't move a muscle. It seemed like Claudia and Courtney were frozen too. Why was everyone being so quiet all of a sudden?

Then Shelby looked at me for the first time since I'd started the mommy joke. Tears welled up in her eyes. "Yeah, I do miss my mom. A lot." Then she slid off the end of the dock into the water.

Alex looked up to see what was going on. "Shelby! Out of the water till it's your turn!" she yelled.

"Sorry, I slipped," Shelby called, bobbing to the surface.

Claudia and Courtney both grabbed me at the same time. "You idiot! Don't you know Shelby's mother is dead?" hissed Claudia.

"Boy, JD! How many signals do I have to give you?" whispered Courtney. "I kept trying to shut you up!"

"Oh," I said.

"I told you to drop it," Claudia went on. "But you just kept going. You really know how to run a joke into the ground."

Shelby was taking her time climbing up the ladder. When she came out, she stood dripping on the end of the dock with her back to us and her arms crossed.

"I didn't know," I whispered to them. We all stared at Mei and Lauren as they finished their exercise with Alex. None of us said anything else. Shelby didn't move.

I sat there with my feet hanging off the edge of the dock, feeling like the biggest jerk in the world. Of course I'd heard their signals. I knew they were trying to shut me up; I just didn't know why. But I kept going. Sometimes when I could tell my jokes weren't funny, I'd get louder instead of letting it drop. Judith was never loud and obnoxious. And she'd never hurt anyone's feelings, either.

Finally Alex made Mei and Lauren get out, and it was Shelby's and my turn. Shelby jumped in, and when she came up, she still wouldn't look at me. I lay down on the dock and reached out to her with my arm first. Shelby swam up and took it quickly.

"Not so fast! Remember—you're in distress and the lifeguard has to help you out," said Alex.

Then I climbed partway down the ladder and offered her my leg. When she was almost up to me, I slid down into the water beside her.

Alex blew her whistle. "No! Stay on the ladder! This is a reaching assist from the side of the pool. Or in this case, a dock."

"Sorry, I slipped!" Then I whispered, "Shelby, I'm sorry." She nodded, but she wouldn't look at me.

Next she swam away from the dock and showed signs of distress, and I had to throw the ring buoy out to her. She grabbed it and I pulled her in.

"Good. Now switch places and Shelby is the rescuer. In the water, JD."

When Shelby climbed out of the water, I whispered to her again. "I didn't know. I never would've said that if I did. Don't you know what JD really stands for? Justa Dimwit." Shelby wiped her bangs out of her eyes and gave me a little smile.

But when I jumped off the end of the dock to be rescued, I had a heavy feeling in my chest, like a weight. I didn't like being boring old Judith. But at times I wasn't crazy about JD, either.

CHAPTER 11

Friday, June 27

"There is no way Alex will make us swim in weather like this!" groaned Mei. "Maybe she'll cancel class."

"Don't count on it," muttered Lauren. It was a foggy, misty morning, and we were all walking to the lake wearing nothing but swimsuits and flip-flops with our towels wrapped around us. Everybody else had left the cabin bundled up in jackets.

"I wish I had a wet suit. The freezing lake water is definitely the worst part of that class," Mei went on.

"No, Alex is the worst part, and I'm the best part!" I shouted. "If I wasn't in this class, you'd all die of boredom!" I twirled around in circles with my towel stretched out like a cape.

Courtney laughed, because she always appreciated

me. I kept spinning in circles as we walked down the gravel road to the lake. "This is fun. I'm getting seriously dizzy. I may puke, and then maybe Alex will excuse me from class."

"No, she'll say, 'Wipe that puke off your chin and jump in the water!'" said Lauren.

I stopped spinning because I saw Natasha and her friend Ashlin walking up behind us. I staggered over and almost crashed right into them.

"Natasha! My first friend!" I threw my arms around her and squeezed her in a bear hug.

"Hi, JD. How are you?" she asked, patting me on the back a little because I wouldn't let her go.

Then I hooked my arm around her shoulder and glared at Ashlin. "How much did you pay Natasha to be her friend?" I demanded. "Five bucks? Or ten? Because she was my friend for free!"

Natasha wriggled away from my arm and patted me on the shoulder. "Calm down, JD. Yes, she's crazy, but she's really harmless," she told Ashlin.

Then Natasha and Ashlin walked away, disappearing into the fog. Natasha always put up with me hugging her all the time and calling her my first friend, but I could tell she was a little tired of my act. Maybe she wasn't the only one. When I didn't get laughs, I never knew what I should do. I wondered if Chloe Carlson ever told jokes that fell flat.

When we got to the lake, mist was rising from the water, making it look spooky and cold. Alex walked up and said in a surprisingly quiet voice, "Lauren, can I talk to you for a second?"

Lauren didn't look at all surprised. In fact, she had an expression on her face like she knew exactly what was coming next. The two of them walked away from us and talked quietly together. Lauren looked small with her towel wrapped around her shoulders.

"What's up?" Claudia whispered, taking a quick peek at her watch.

"I don't know, but I don't think it's good," Courtney whispered back.

"She'd better be nice to her, or I'll give her a knuckle sandwich," I murmured. We all whispered to each other and kept our eyes down, not daring to look in their direction. Every single one of us tried to act like we didn't know what was going on.

Then Lauren looked at us before she walked away from the lake. Alex came toward the rest of us with a frown on her face. "Okay, ladies. Today I want to work on CPR," she informed us, her voice still soft. She walked over to a storage shed near the end of the lake.

We all looked at each other but kept quiet. Everyone was so serious. It was like someone had died.

Alex came back, dragging a dummy under one arm. It had a head, arms, and a body but no legs. She stretched it out in front of our little semicircle.

"This is Clyde P. Ripple," she said. "Clyde has just been pulled from the water and is unresponsive. I've alerted another lifeguard to call 911. Now I'm going to check to see if Clyde is breathing." She knelt over the dummy.

"Poor Clyde!" I wailed. "Looks like another shark attack victim!" The whole group was so gloomy, I figured I had to liven things up. Mei and Courtney snickered and looked away.

"He's not breathing," said Alex in a loud voice, like she hadn't heard me, "so now I'll begin to administer CPR. I first check for foreign objects in his mouth."

"Spit out your gum, Clyde!" I whispered loudly.

Alex's lips pressed into a thin line. "Then I tilt his head back to open his airway."

"I hope Clyde's a good kisser," I said.

"JD, shut up," said Alex. "Now I'll do two puffs of air and turn my head to watch his chest rise."

"If Clyde doesn't make it, let's have a burial at sea," I suggested.

Alex stopped and looked at me. "You're about to push me too far. This is your second warning."

"Ruh-roh, Raggy!" I said in my best Scooby-Doo voice.

"This is CPR, JD. This is a lifesaving procedure. Not only are you missing out on all this information, but you're preventing the rest of the girls in class from learning it too. If I hear one more crack out of you, you're gonna leave and not come back." Alex stared me down and I kept quiet. Then she turned her attention back to Clyde.

"Crack," I whispered to Courtney, just to get in the last word. I truly didn't think Alex would hear me, or maybe I thought she'd ignore me like she often tried to do.

Alex stood up and pointed. "Leave. You're out of this class. I don't want to see you back here again."

Nobody looked at me, and I didn't look at them, either. Everything was deathly quiet. I stood up and wrapped my towel around me. Alex still pointed, like I'd asked her for directions and she needed to show me the way. I walked away from the group; the only sound I could hear was my flip-flops smacking against the wet grass. I walked past the shallow end of the lake where Isabel was taking her swimming lesson. Hardly anyone was out in canoes this morning, partly because of the weather, and partly because a group was leaving soon for a river trip.

For the first time all summer, I was by myself. The only time I was ever completely by myself was in the showers or in Solitary, but even then somebody was usually in the stall beside me. I walked back up the gravel road, past the dining hall, and then up the hill toward the Middler cabins. I didn't see any other campers wandering around because everyone was at activities. The fog was starting to lift, but the whole camp still felt quiet and deserted.

At least I could go back to the cabin and change into some warm clothes. Lauren was probably there, and we could cabin-sit for the rest of the morning. I couldn't wait to tell her I'd been kicked out of class too. Maybe it would make her feel better. Why couldn't the two of us have switched places? Lauren really wanted to do well, but she wasn't a good enough swimmer. I couldn't have cared less, and yet everything we did was easy for me. It wasn't fair.

I passed Middler Lodge, where we had evening programs every night after dinner. It was empty now, and the big doors stood open. I didn't really care that I'd been kicked out. I never wanted to do that class in the first place. I only took it to be with my friends. All those girls were hoping to be lifeguards some day. Not me.

When I got to our cabin, at first I thought nobody was there. Lauren wasn't on Side A, which meant she must've changed clothes and then left for some other activity. Too bad, because I'd really wanted to talk to her. I opened my trunk to find some clothes.

"What are you doing here?"

I turned around to see Katherine standing in the entry way. "I could ask you the same question," I said, turning my back on her so I could change.

"I thought you had that swim class."

"I used to. Alex kicked me out." I pulled a sweatshirt over my head.

"How come? What'd you do?" asked Katherine.

"Nothing. I made Alex mad. I kept telling jokes and wouldn't shut up."

Katherine made a snorting sound. "It figures. Look, let me give you some advice. You're always trying to be funny, but you're not. You put on this big act like you're a real troublemaker—getting caught by the Porch Patrol and all that. Big whoop. You're trying to be something you're not."

I closed my trunk but didn't turn around. It was like Katherine had read my mind. What else did she know about me?

"At least everyone likes me," I said over my shoulder. "My whole cabin hasn't turned against me." From Day One, Katherine had been hard to get along with, and then she'd started teasing Isabel because she couldn't swim. Now none of us could stand her.

"Oh, boo-hoo, I'm so sad that I don't have any friends," said Katherine, wandering back over to Side B. She was obviously annoyed that I'd interrupted her morning of cabin-sitting all by herself. I was glad she was going to leave me alone.

I climbed up on my top bunk and stretched out. *You're always trying to be funny, but you're not.* Partly that was just Katherine being her crabby self. But then maybe part of it was true. I'd seen other people roll their eyes when I cracked jokes. And this morning even Natasha seemed tired of my act; she'd always liked me before.

I turned over on my side and stared at the wall. JD WAS HERE. I'd written that last Sunday, the day after the dance, when everyone was still talking about me and Lance. I was feeling pretty darn good about myself then. I reached out and touched the rough wood of the cabin wall.

I'd been able to keep up the JD act for almost two whole weeks. But now everything was falling apart. I got on people's nerves, I hurt people's feelings, I tried to be the life of the party, but instead I just made a fool of myself.

And I'd finally pushed Alex too far. Why didn't I keep my mouth shut? I'd wanted to get one more laugh in. And maybe part of me wanted Alex to kick me out. Now I could finally do the activities I really wanted to do, since Guard Start wouldn't be taking up all my time.

But then I'd also written my family about the class and told them how good I was. I didn't even have to lie about that part; it was true. And Michelle had told them the same thing in the letter she'd sent. What was I supposed to tell them now? *Oh yeah, you know that pre-lifeguarding class I was taking? I got kicked out for cracking jokes, so I didn't finish it.* How was I ever going to explain that? *But Judith, that's so unlike you.* And did my parents really need another kid disappointing them? Hadn't they already been through enough with Justin?

I grabbed my pillow and buried my face in it. As much as I hated to admit it, Katherine was right about one thing. So much for trying to be something I wasn't. I should've known this would never last. Maybe it was time for me to make JD disappear.

"JD!" Courtney and Mei came bursting through the screen door looking for me. I'd been waiting for them. I knew they'd come looking for me as soon as class ended.

"Hi." I sat up on my top bunk and looked at them. Courtney had a *what am I going to do with you* look on her face. Mei stood there with her arms crossed.

"We've got to fix this," said Courtney. "It's bad enough we lost Lauren. We can't lose you, too."

"I've got to tell . . ." *I've got to tell you guys something. My name's really Judith. And before camp, I had the personality of a doorknob. My brain's worn out from thinking up jokes. I'm going back to my old self. Maybe you'll like me or maybe you won't.*

"Yes! That's exactly what I was thinking! You've got to tell Alex you're sorry. If you apologize to her, maybe she'll let you back in the class," Courtney suggested.

"Hey, where's Lauren?" asked Mei. "We need to talk to her, too."

"I haven't seen her," I said. I cleared my throat and tried to start again. "Listen. I have a confession to make."

The screen door banged open and Lauren walked in. She was wearing the same shorts with "Dancer" across the backside that she'd worn the first day. She climbed up to her top bunk, then propped her chin on her hands and stared at all of us. "Well, go ahead and ask. I know you're all dying to know."

"Okay," said Mei, leaning against the metal bunk frame and looking up at her. "What did Alex say to you?"

Lauren let out a sigh. "Actually, she was really nice to me, if you can believe it. She said I was doing great with all the service hours and workbook activities, but she didn't think I'd be able to swim five hundred yards. Big surprise."

"Was that all?" Courtney asked.

"She said I could keep coming to class to learn as much as I could, or I could try again next summer."

She tugged on her blond ponytail and shrugged. "It's nothing I didn't already know. I've been worried about passing that test since the first day. Now I'm off the hook." She picked up her pillow and hugged it.

"Well, guess what?" I said. "I'm out of the class too. I finally pushed Alex over the edge."

"What happened?"

Everyone was looking at me. "We were all mad about the way she treated you, and so Alex was standing at the end of the dock watching everyone in the water. I walked up behind her . . . and pushed her over the edge!"

Lauren hid her smile behind her pillow.

"Yeah, she was blowing her whistle at me the whole way in, but as soon as she hit the water, it got water-logged and only made a noise like this." I made wet raspberry noises with my lips. By now, all three of them were laughing.

"So then she swam over and tried to climb up the ladder, but I planted my foot right on her forehead and said, 'Oh, no you don't!'" I stuck out my foot to demonstrate how I'd kicked the imaginary Alex back under.

"So then she was fighting mad. I jumped in and landed on her back, and she kept trying to throw me off, but I hung on for dear life. Then Courtney got on

Mei's back, and Shelby got on Claudia's, and we had the most vicious chicken fights you've ever seen in your life." Courtney and Mei were actually bent over laughing now. "Sorry you missed it, Lauren. It was actually a pretty useful class. Alex and I won, by the way. Then she kicked me out."

"Shut up! You guys aren't the only people in this cabin, you know!" yelled Katherine from Side B, because we were all laughing so loud.

"Sorry, Katherine! I'm just over here NOT being funny, and everyone's laughing at how NOT funny I am!" I shouted. Okay, maybe I'd been a little hard on myself. On JD. She seemed to be her old self again. Or was that her new self?

There was a tap at the door. "Hey. JD? Courtney?" A face pressed against the screen. It was Shelby, and Claudia was with her.

Mei ran over and opened the door for them. "We have visitors!"

Claudia and Shelby came in. "JD, you have to apologize to Alex. She'll probably let you back in if you settle down. You're the best swimmer in the class," said Claudia, and Shelby nodded.

Wow! I couldn't believe it. I'd always thought I'd gotten on Claudia's nerves, and I didn't think Shelby was too crazy about me either since that stupid mommy song.

"Nah, she hates me. She's hated me since the swim tests, when I yelled 'shark!' She's glad to get rid of me."

"Are you okay?" Shelby asked, looking up at Lauren.

"Oh, sure. I'm a lousy swimmer, but I'm okay."

"You're not a lousy swimmer. And you're a great dancer," said Courtney.

Lauren looked at her and grinned. "Well, that part is true."

"So are you going to do it?" asked Shelby, looking up at me on my bunk. "If you apologize and you're really sincere, she'll probably give you a second chance."

"Why should she? I've been wasting her time all summer," I told them all.

"Because despite what a hardnose she is, she's all about swimming. And you are definitely her star student when it comes to skills," Claudia explained.

"It's true," agreed Courtney. "Look, at the very least, you kinda owe her an apology anyway. What's the worst thing that could happen? She turns you down, and you're still out of the class. But maybe this way, you might get back in."

It was great that they all wanted me to come back. It made me feel wanted—which, considering the way I'd been feeling an hour ago, was pretty nice.

But a part of me felt the same way Lauren did. Now I was off the hook for the class and I didn't have to go anymore. No more icy plunges first thing in the morning. No more spending all my mornings at the lake helping out with swim lessons to do all my service hours. No more wasting my time pretending I was really interested in becoming a lifeguard. I hardly had any time for tennis or rappelling and rock climbing, all the other stuff I'd so wanted to try.

They were all looking at me with these puppy-dog eyes.

"Do it," urged Lauren. "You are the best swimmer."

"Okay, okay! I'll do it for my fans!" I said, sliding down from my bunk and taking bows left and right.

Then I grabbed Courtney's shoulders. "But there's one thing I have to know. Clyde? Did he make it? Did he pull through?"

Courtney clapped me on the shoulder and shook her head. "I'm afraid not. We buried him at sea, just like you requested."

I collapsed on the floor and bawled fake tears. But I hadn't been this happy since the Porch Patrol incident.

CHAPTER 13

Saturday, June 28

"Now's your chance!" Courtney whispered to me as she brushed her hair.

"No! We'll be late for assembly!" I whispered back. I was putting away my toothbrush after brushing my teeth in Solitary.

"You're stalling!" she hissed at me.

"Okay, fine. I'll try to talk to her, but don't be surprised if she brushes me off."

The bell had just rung for assembly on the hill. The whole camp was supposed to be there for the flag raising.

Courtney gave me a stern look as she walked out the door. Lauren and Mei had already left. Alex, Isabel, and I were the only ones still in the cabin.

"Uh, Alex?" I asked, walking over to Side B. "Could I please talk to you for a second?"

"Now? It's time for assembly." She was changing clothes after coming back from her Friday night leave. All the counselors got one night off every week. It was the first chance I'd had to talk to her since class yesterday.

"It's really important," I told her.

Alex glanced at Isabel tying her shoes. "You'd better go. You're going to be late."

Isabel rushed out the door and left us alone in the cabin.

"Let's go. You can talk to me on the way," she said. We walked out together. Alex walked fast, and I had to hurry to keep up.

"Um, I want to apologize for yesterday," I started off. "I know I've caused a lot of trouble in class. And yesterday was really bad." We turned by Middler Lodge, and we could see the whole camp already sitting in the grass out on the hill. The flag raising hadn't started yet.

"I know CPR is really important. I shouldn't have been goofing off and distracting everybody while you were trying to teach it." There, that sounded pretty good. And it was even sincere.

"Okay," said Alex. She'd slowed down, but she hadn't really looked at me yet.

"I know I've been a real slacker. I'm sorry about that. You *are* a good teacher." I hadn't planned on saying that last part, but then I realized it was true. She was strict, and most of the time I didn't like her, but she was doing a good job.

"I really have learned a lot in the class. We all have. You obviously really care about teaching us the right methods."

Alex stopped walking and looked at me. "Yes, I do. And you've been one frustration after another for me, JD."

"I know. I'm sorry." Now I really did feel bad about being such a troublemaker. My number-one goal had been to get laughs and make everyone think I was this amazingly funny and popular person. I'd never really thought about how much harder I made her job.

Eda, the camp director, was walking up the hill with the CATs who were about to raise the flag. It was a good thing there wasn't underwear up the flagpole like there had been a few days ago. When I saw it, I was so bummed I hadn't thought of doing something funny like that.

"Is there any way you'd let me back in the class?" I blurted out. "I promise I'll totally calm down and won't cause any more trouble at all. I swear!" I crossed my heart to show her how much I meant it.

Alex edged down the hill closer to the rest of the crowd, and I followed her. She let out a long, tired sigh. "You know, this all sounds really nice and sincere, but I'm not sure I can trust you to behave. So far, you've shown me nothing but disrespect. You hardly ever listen, you crack jokes when I'm talking. You don't act at all interested in really learning anything, JD."

Well, she had me there. "You're right. I wasn't really that into the class. I mainly took it to be with my friends. But now I'd like to try to finish it. I'm pretty good, I think."

"Everyone please stand for the flag raising," announced Eda, and so we had to shut up. I still wasn't completely convinced I wanted to spend even more time on the class. But at least I'd done what the others wanted me to do. I did apologize. And I did ask to get back in.

Alex and I stood at the back of the crowd and watched while the CATs raised the flag. Then we had to say the pledge. When we were done, everyone sat down, and Eda began the announcements.

"We'll talk about this when assembly's over," Alex told me. Then she moved over to where Libby and some of the other swimming counselors were sitting, leaving me stuck all by myself. Courtney, Mei, and Lauren were way in the front. I saw Courtney looking around for me in the crowd, but she didn't see me back here.

Saturday was the only day the whole camp got together for an assembly. Besides Eda's announcements, different counselors stood up to let people know about upcoming trips out of camp. I sat there and listened and wondered what Alex would decide.

When assembly ended, I moved through the crowd and met up with everyone else.

"Did you talk to her?" asked Courtney.

"Yeah. I apologized. And I even asked if I could get back in, so I hope you're happy."

"Well, what did she say?" Mei asked.

I rolled my eyes. "She didn't. The flag raising started and we had to stop talking. She *said* she'd talk to me about it later."

"There she is! Go talk to her now!" Mei gave me a push in Alex's direction.

I walked over and stood near Alex, waiting for her to finish her conversation with the rest of the swimming counselors. When she was done, she looked at me.

"I guess you want an answer." She frowned at me.

"If you just give me another chance, I swear I'll really change." We walked away with the rest of the crowd. Everyone was scattering in different directions.

"I want to talk to you about something," said Alex.

"Okay," I agreed, feeling a little nervous. We were approaching Middler Lodge, and Alex motioned me to follow her.

"In here," she said.

The lodge was a big stone building with high ceilings and wooden rafters, a moose head over the fireplace, and a wide porch around the outside. Alex made me sit down on a wooden bench, but she stood the whole time.

"You're the worst possible student a teacher could have."

I'd always known she didn't like me, but I didn't think she hated me that much. How was I supposed to respond to that?

"You know why?"

"No," I said. I'd always thought I was at least good at the swimming part, even if I sucked at the listening part.

"Because, JD, of all the students in the class, you have the most potential. But you're the biggest screwup. I'd rather have ten Laurens who can't swim more than a hundred yards but who really care about the class and give it their all."

"I know." I looked down at my hands. I knew that what she was saying was true.

"You're the best swimmer in your class, and I think you're probably better than the group of Senior girls I'm teaching too, and they're all a year or two older than you. I've seen fifteen-year-olds in lifeguarding classes who aren't as strong as you are."

"Really?" I knew I was good, but I had no idea I was *that* good.

"Absolutely. But so far I haven't seen any desire from you at all. I wish I could take your skills and give them to Lauren, because she had more desire than anyone."

"I know!" I said, looking up at her. "That's just how I felt yesterday morning!"

"So if I let you back in, what's going to happen?"

"I'll stop causing trouble. I'll listen—for once."

Alex shook her head and sighed. "I would love for you to finish the class."

"Really?" I'd figured she was glad to get rid of me.

"Of course. I want everyone to finish. I'd hoped Lauren would at least stay in and keep learning, but she decided she'd rather wait till next year to try the class again. And that's okay. All I want to do is to prepare every single person in my class to become a good lifeguard."

"I promise—you won't even recognize me in class from now on. It'll be like I'm a completely different person," I managed to say with a straight face.

Alex raised her eyebrows. "Okay. But one tiny slip-up, and I don't ever want to see your face again."

"Thanks, Alex!" She let me go, and I raced up the steps toward our cabin. Everyone else would be happy to hear the news. And I was good at something, really good. Wouldn't my parents be thrilled when I wrote them about that?

Monday, June 30

"Today we're going to do a submerged rescue," said Alex. "What do you think that means?"

"When you're under the water?" guessed Mei.

"Well, yes. It's when your drowning victim has gone under, and you have to go underwater to complete the rescue." Alex kept talking, explaining how this was different from a rescue where the victim was splashing around and still conscious. I sat quietly and listened.

For once I felt like I could relax. I didn't have to be "on" the whole time, trying to come up with a joke. Everyone knew I was on probation, and one slip-up would get me kicked out again. It was great to finally have an excuse to be good.

Alex demonstrated how we were supposed to swim

down to our victim and wrap the rescue tube around her before bringing her up to the surface.

"Okay, let's pair up. One of you will be the victim, and the other is the rescuer. If you're the victim, I want you to go under toward the bottom of the lake and then float there. When the rescuer approaches you, stay passive, like you're unconscious."

Claudia threw me a quick glance, like she expected me to make a joke about that. I looked back at her with my lips pressed together as if they were glued shut.

Shelby and Courtney were the first ones to try it. Shelby dove in, came up for a quick breath, and then did a surface dive. Courtney stayed on the dock, holding the red foam rescue tube and waiting until Alex blew her whistle. Then she wrapped the tube around her waist and jumped in.

Alex had told us that the tricky part would be forcing the tube underwater. It was made to float, and so it took a lot of strength to get it to submerge. We watched Courtney struggle with it. She looked like she was wrestling a giant hot dog. Meanwhile, poor Shelby was probably turning blue near the bottom of the lake.

After a couple of minutes Shelby bobbed to the surface and took a breath. "What's going on?" she asked.

"Sorry. This is really hard," said Courtney.

Alex told Shelby to get out for a few seconds while she jumped in and showed Courtney how to submerge the tube. But even after watching Alex, Courtney still had trouble doing it.

"Okay, let's mix things up a little." Alex climbed up the ladder and handed me the tube. "Courtney, this time I want you to be the victim."

Courtney dove under and stayed there. Alex signaled me to jump in and save her. I wrapped the tube around my waist and jumped in, bobbing up again quickly because the tube made me float. Then I pulled the tube into the water vertically the way Alex had shown Courtney.

The tube started to float back up, but I forced it down with all my strength. Once I had the whole thing below the surface, it was a little easier to control. I kept a firm grip on it while I swam down to where Courtney was floating.

Now the tricky part was getting the tube in between me and Courtney. It kept trying to float up to the surface. And I could only hold on to the tube with one hand because I had to grab Courtney with my other arm. After a few seconds I had the tube in place, and I swam back up to the surface, bringing my victim along with me.

When we both came up, everyone applauded and cheered. "Excellent! That's exactly how it's done!" said Alex.

Then she made me get out and demonstrate to everyone how I'd done it. I felt pretty good that I'd done it right the first time. After I gave them all a few tips, she sent Mei and Claudia in to try it. Mei was the rescuer, and she had as much trouble getting the tube under as Courtney had.

In fact, everyone had a hard time with this exercise. It was one of the hardest things we'd done so far. Every time someone was struggling, Alex told me to get in and show them how to do it. At first I thought it was pretty cool that she was asking me to show everyone how to submerge the tube. But then it occurred to me: She wasn't letting me help her teach the class. She was being especially hard on me to make sure I knew she was the boss. It didn't take long till I was completely exhausted.

So this was how it was going to be. She'd let me back in the class, but she was going to torture me the whole time. Why did I want to put myself through this?

"Okay. That's enough for today. I'll see you guys during free swim, right?" Alex asked us as we got our towels and dried ourselves off. She expected all of us to show up later to do some of our service hours, helping the swim staff lifeguard during free swim.

"Yes," Shelby and Courtney replied. The rest of us groaned.

We were walking away when Alex called me back. "JD, I want to talk to you for a minute." My shoulders slumped. Why couldn't she leave me alone?

When Mei and Courtney tried to hang around and wait for me, Alex told them I would catch up with them later, so they left me alone with her.

"You thought I was pretty hard on you today, didn't you?" she asked me.

"Yes," I said, looking her in the eye. I had to obey her. I didn't have to like her.

"You know why I asked so much of you?"

"To keep me in line. Maybe to punish me a little for causing trouble in the past."

"No, that's not it at all. You're the only one who could do that exercise so easily. Maybe I do expect more of you, but that's because you can do more. I doubt Mei ever would've been able to submerge that tube if you hadn't kept showing her how."

I didn't say anything. "Well, that's all I wanted to say. You did a great job today. For the first time you performed up to the level of your ability."

Then she let me go. As I walked away, I couldn't help smiling. Now I knew how Justin and Adam must feel, being the best at something. When camp was over, I could brag to both of them about what a great swimmer I was. I knew they'd be proud of me.

But then I wondered, would hearing about my great success make Justin feel even worse about his own problems?

CHAPTER 15

Friday, July 4

"Every cabin needs to enter at least one act. You've got almost a whole week to get ready, but first you guys should decide who's going to enter," said Michelle.

"I nominate JD!" Courtney called out.

"Great idea! She'd be perfect!" said Amber.

"Wait a second, you guys!" I told them. "I didn't agree to this."

"Oh, JD, you'd be great!" exclaimed Michelle. "What kind of act are you going to do?"

"Something funny," Amber said. "If JD's doing it, it'll definitely be funny."

One minute Michelle was explaining to us that a talent show was coming up next week. The next minute *I'd* been picked to represent the whole cabin.

"Are any of you guys talented?" I asked, jumping up on Michelle's bed and looking over at Side B.

"Not me." Isabel shook her head.

"I can whistle," said Meredith.

"I could do impressions of all the people in camp I hate," offered Katherine.

"You do it, JD," said Mei. "You're the obvious choice."

I plopped down on Michelle's bed. "What if I don't want to? What if I say no?"

"Well, somebody needs to step up, because every cabin is supposed to participate. So be thinking about it. Make it fun," Michelle said. "Now all you guys need to go to the dining hall so Alex and I can hide."

On the way to the dining hall we saw a bunch of counselors wandering around. They were waiting for us to go inside before they went to their hiding places.

The best part about the Fourth of July was that we didn't have any regular activities all day, which meant we got a day off from Guard Start. This morning we'd had a capture-the-flag game with the Juniors and Middlers playing against the Seniors. We won. Now it was time for the counselor hunt.

Inside the dining hall Eda explained the rules to us. "Counselors can hide anywhere on the camp property, but they cannot leave camp. No hiding in the stables, either, because it bothers the horses. Each counselor is worth a certain number of points based on how many years she's been at Pine Haven. When someone in your cabin catches a counselor, tell her your cabin number so you'll get credit for those points. Once a counselor is caught, she'll come back here to the dining hall. The cabin with the most points wins."

Then Eda made us sing three or four camp songs to give the counselors plenty of time to hide. Some of the camp songs I actually liked, but one of them that Eda made us sing was so sappy and stupid, it always made us laugh. It was called "Camp Days!" and it was to the tune of "My Bonnie Lies Over the Ocean."

> *Pine Haven, we'll always remember*
> *For friendships so wholesome and true.*
> *Pine Haven, you gave us our girlhood,*
> *Forever, we'll love only you!*
> *Camp Days! Camp Days! We frolic and skip in the*
> *dew, the dew!*
> *Camp Days! Camp Days! We frolic and skip in the*
> *dew!*
> *Your mountains inspire us to greatness,*
> *Your streams fill our pure hearts with song,*

Your trees make our souls sing with rapture,
Pine Haven, to you we belong!

When we got to the chorus about frolicking and skipping in the dew, I held my arms over my head and did some funky moves to make everyone laugh.

Pine Haven, when we have to leave you,
The sorrow we feel will be great.
Our hearts pine for you all the winter,
Pine Haven, to us you're first-rate!

Mei had her hands over her ears when we sang the chorus for the last time. "That's the stupidest song ever. Where did it even come from?"

"I think someone made it up about seventy years ago," I told her. Eda opened the dining hall doors, and we all rushed outside.

"We should split up," suggested Lauren. "We'll cover more ground that way."

"Good plan. Plus it's hard for eight people to stay together," I said.

"How about the little Guard Start clique all stay together, and the rest of us rejects will be another group," Katherine said, wiping sweat off her forehead and flicking it at Isabel. It was a hot, sunny afternoon, and already we were all red-faced and sweaty.

"I'm not in the Guard Start class any more, Katherine. So I guess I'm with you rejects," said Lauren. She took a couple of steps toward Katherine, who backed away.

"No one's a reject," Meredith said. "Look, these are the teams. Me, Amber, Katherine, and JD will be together, and Isabel, Lauren, Courtney, and Mei in the other group. And remember, we're all working together for Cabin Two, right?"

We all agreed that was a good way to split up the cabin. It evenly divided the A and B sides and broke up our "little Guard Start clique." And it kept Isabel and Katherine apart. Meredith was the best. She'd probably grow up to be a hostage negotiator.

"I know a great spot where a bunch of counselors always hide," Amber told us. "Over in the woods near the camp store." So our group took off in that direction, with Amber leading the way.

I knew it wasn't any big deal, but I couldn't stop thinking about the talent show next week. Had I really been picked to do an act for it? It was pretty cool that everyone automatically pointed to me and said I should be the one to do it. That never would've happened to Judith.

"Do you guys really think I should be in the talent show?" I asked. "Be honest. Because if somebody else wants to do an act, I don't mind."

"I think you're perfect for the talent show, JD. You have the best sense of humor of anyone in the cabin," said Amber.

"Yeah, you do it. Nobody else wants to," said Katherine as we walked along. The sunshine made everything look wavy, like a mirage. "If you guys really want to catch some people, we should hotwire one of the counselors' cars and drive downtown to Sonic. Half of them are down there now drinking cherry limeades while we get heat stroke looking for them."

"They can't leave camp, Katherine," Meredith reminded her.

"They cheat, you lamebrain. Some people never get found. Caroline Heyward? She's worth fourteen points, and nobody's ever found her. Why? Because she and a bunch of counselors jump in their cars and leave camp before we're even out of the dining hall."

"But what kind of act should I do?" I asked. I felt like everyone had dropped the talent show in my lap and told me to figure it out for myself.

"You'll think of something. It'll be great. Don't worry about it," Meredith assured me. "I hope we find Alex and

Michelle. Together they're worth seventeen points."

We were at the edge of the woods now, and Katherine was complaining about ticks. "Just what I need—a raging case of Lyme disease."

"Oh, don't think of the woods like that," said Amber. "'Deep green in summer, golden in fall / Barest in winter, spring blooms for all.' That's how I like to think of the woods." We crept through the underbrush, keeping our eyes out for any signs of people hiding.

"That's nice. Where'd you hear that?" I asked her.

"Oh, that? Uh, I made it up. It's part of a poem I wrote about trees." She blushed a little. Amber spent almost every rest hour either reading poetry or writing some of her own. I'd never thought of writing poetry as something to do for fun.

"I see someone!" yelled Meredith. We crashed through tree branches and caught Gloria, a counselor who worked in the Crafts Cabin. She'd been hiding behind a vine-covered tree stump.

"We got you! Middler Cabin Two. How many points are you worth?" I asked her, as she stood up and brushed leaves out of her hair.

"Uh, just one," she said. "This is my first year." She gave us a little smile, like she was sorry she wasn't worth more.

Gloria walked away to report back to the dining hall, and Katherine nodded knowingly. "See. The rookies don't know any better. They actually hide in camp. One lousy point. What a waste of time."

"Shut up, Miss Sunshine!" I snapped at her, but Meredith quieted me down and we kept looking.

Our group actually did pretty well overall. We found five counselors who totaled twenty-two points. At five o'clock the bell rang, and we all went back to the dining hall.

"We caught four people," Mei announced when we met up with the other half of Cabin 2. "They were worth nineteen points."

"Cool, that gives us a grand total of forty-one," said Meredith. But it still wasn't enough to beat out Senior Cabin 7, which won with fifty points.

"Senior Cabin 7 will be first in line for ice cream at dinner," announced Eda to the whole dining hall. "And tomorrow you can all sleep late, because you get a day off from inspection!" They all cheered while the rest of us groaned in envy. Getting a day off from cleaning the cabin was one of the best rewards to get. Our cabin kept getting demerits during inspection, thanks to Katherine.

Nobody found Caroline Heyward, the counselor worth fourteen points, but Michelle got caught down near the archery range by Junior Cabin 3, and Middler Cabin 1 found Alex near the campfire circle, so at least we knew *our* counselors hadn't cheated.

There was a big fireworks show planned for that night, so instead of eating in the dining hall, we had dinner out on the hill—hot dogs, baked beans, chips, and lemonade in little Styrofoam cups. A lot of campers were already lined up in front of the long food tables, and others sat around in groups in the grass, eating off paper plates. Once we got our food, we all found spots in the grass to sit down.

I couldn't stop thinking about what Michelle had said earlier.

"Hey, guys. About the talent show Michelle mentioned. Am I . . ."

"Yes, you're doing it," said Courtney, like that was the end of the discussion. She reached down and carefully picked up a ladybug from a blade of grass.

"Well, okay. But what should I do?" No one but me seemed to consider this a big deal.

"Whatever you want to do. You'll come up with a great idea, JD. You've got such a fabulous sense of humor," Courtney assured me. She blew softly on the ladybug, and it opened its wings and flew away.

"I could use some help. Maybe all four of us could

do something together. We just need to think of something." After all, Michelle hadn't said only one person had to do the act. Doing it as a group would be a lot better. At least some of the pressure would be off me that way.

"I get stage fright," said Mei, licking the barbecue seasoning off her chip before popping it into her mouth.

"And I'm not funny," Lauren put in.

"Well, it doesn't have to be funny, does it?" I pointed out. "We could do . . ." My brain strained to think of what kind of act the four of us could do, but nothing came to me.

"Yeah, but funny is best. Funny always works," said Mei. "My school has a talent show every year, and sure, some kids play the violin or sing, but the acts people remember are the funny ones."

"Like what? I really need some ideas."

"You'll think of something. You've got a whole week to plan it," said Courtney.

"Yeah, it'll be great. I bet Cabin Two wins the talent show with JD as our act," Mei predicted. "Then maybe we'll get a day off from inspection like those Seniors in Cabin Seven."

I had this horrible tense feeling in the pit of my stomach. It was like a teacher had just announced a big research project due next week, and half our grade was riding on it.

How would I ever come up with an idea? And what if I couldn't think of anything? Then what? I could see myself up on a stage, standing all alone in a spotlight with a silent audience staring at me, waiting for me to do something. *Something funny*. But my mouth felt like it was full of cotton, and my feet were two lead weights, glued to the stage.

I was going to bomb. There was no doubt about it.

Saturday, July 5

"Come on. We're your friends. You *have* to tell us," pleaded Mei.

"There's no secret to it, really," I said. "Just walk up to one of them and start talking. That's all I did the last time." I glanced at my reflection in the little mirror on the wall. We were all making last-minute touch-ups before leaving for the dining hall. Tonight was the second dance with Camp Crockett. This time the boys were coming to Pine Haven. I was just glad to have a break from worrying about the talent show for a while. And I was looking forward to seeing Lance again.

"But what did you say to them? You had to talk to them about *something*." Mei kept pumping me.

"You're definitely holding out on us," said Lauren. "I

helped you guys with some dance moves. The least you could do is tell us how you got all those boys to start talking."

All afternoon my friends had been trying to get me to reveal my secret. It was fun to keep them all guessing. It was like being the only one who knew a cheat code to a game that would get me to a certain level. If I kept it a secret, I would continue to amaze them with my abilities. On the other hand, if I did tell them, they'd all be grateful.

"Okay, you guys. I'll tell you. But don't go telling everyone. There's one subject all boys are interested in," I announced. They all stopped primping and looked at me.

"Sports?" asked Lauren.

"Girls?" guessed Mei.

"No. I mean, lots of them are interested in sports and girls, but the one thing that all boys are into"—I paused for effect—"is . . . video games."

"Video games?" Courtney said. "*That's* your secret?"

"But I don't know anything about video games!" Mei groaned.

"Start off by asking them what systems they own and what their favorite games are," I told her. "Then ask them what games they want to buy. All guys have a video game wish list." I gave them a quick briefing about systems and games. They didn't really need to know that much, as long as they could ask the right questions.

"We'd better go," said Courtney. "A lot of girls are already down there." We left the cabin and walked down the hill toward the dining hall.

"So what are you and Lance planning this time?" asked Lauren. "If you elope, should we write to your parents and tell them?"

I tried to think of something funny to say, but I was stumped. A few people had been teasing me, asking if I was going to get caught by the Porch Patrol again. I didn't really know what to say. How was I supposed to top getting caught during the last dance? That was the trouble with having a reputation: People expected a lot from you.

"I have to behave myself tonight," I said finally. "Michelle warned me to be good." That part was true. After the first dance, Michelle had pulled me aside and grilled me about what Lance and I had been up to. I'd sworn to her that he hadn't laid a hand on me, that we'd just talked about video games all night and he'd offered to show me his *Tips & Tricks* magazine. She hadn't looked very happy with me, though, and today she'd told me not to pull any "stunts" like last time.

"I thought you said this guy kissed like a fish," said Mei. "Do you really want to see him again?"

"Yeah, I do. He happens to be a very nice guy," I said, regretting my fish pucker joke. Tonight my goal was to get Lance to slow dance with me. And not because I wanted to impress everyone. Last time I'd been so concerned about working on my reputation, I hadn't even danced a single dance. Tonight that was going to change.

Inside the dining hall we had to wait around for the boys to arrive. When they started coming in, I looked for Lance, but he wasn't the first guy I saw.

Brandon Matheson came walking in with a group of boys who must have been from his cabin. As soon as I saw him, I stepped behind Courtney. I hoped her hair would hide me, and it did a little, but it didn't help that I was a head taller than she was.

Brandon! I hadn't even thought about him. I'd have to dodge that chatterbox all night! I pretended I was scratching my forehead and managed to peek through my fingers in his direction. He wasn't looking over here. The last thing I needed was for him to start talking to me again when all my friends were around.

"JD, there he is!" said Courtney, and for a second I thought she was talking about Brandon. But it was Lance she was pointing to.

"Let's go tell him he kisses like a fish!" said Mei, really loud.

I grabbed both her arms and squeezed. "Don't you dare! I'll never speak to you again! *And* I won't tell you any more stuff about video games."

Mei burst out laughing and wriggled away from me. "Calm down. I'm just joking with you."

Courtney and Lauren were laughing too. "I've never seen you so worried, JD. It's not like you," Courtney said.

I was about to snap at them all, *Maybe you don't know me as well as you think.* But I stopped myself and tried to act casual. "Look, I'm gonna go say hi to him. If you need any help, just come ask me."

I left them and squeezed through the crowd of people to get to Lance. He was with Mike and David again, and when they saw me walking toward them, David punched Lance in the arm.

"Hi, guys," I said.

They all said hi. Lance smiled, and his dimple appeared in his cheek. I loved that dimple. And I noticed something else about him. The reason he had such gorgeous eyes was that he had really long eyelashes. I wondered what he'd look like without his glasses. I was glad to see that tonight he'd actually combed his hair—no more bed head.

We talked for a few minutes, and then luckily, David and Mike walked off. Lance and I found some chairs to sit in on the edge of the dance floor.

"Hey, do you like the *Ratchet and Clank* games?" asked Lance.

"Sure, I've played the first one, Going Commando, and Size Matters. Which one's your favorite?" I asked him.

The only problem with getting guys on the subject of video games was figuring out how to get them off it later. We talked about *Ratchet & Clank* for about ten minutes until Courtney came over.

"JD, I need to talk to you!" She insisted that we talk in private.

"What does WoW mean? This guy keeps talking to me about it," she whispered when we'd walked away from where Lance was sitting.

"Oh, that's *World of Warcraft*. It's an online game. You play it with other people online, and tons of people are really into it. Some even get addicted."

Courtney let out a sigh. "Okay, thanks. At least I know what the heck he's talking about now." She walked off, and I went back to Lance.

But then less than two minutes later, Mei found me because *she* had a question. "Hey, JD—what's FPS?"

"That's first-person shooter. It's a game where you see everything through a character's eyes, but you don't actually see the character himself. The other type is third-person shooter. In those games you can see the character onscreen," I explained.

"Oh, I get it. Thanks!" Then Mei looked over to where Lance was sitting and said, "Hey, Lance, JD says you're a . . ." She looked at me with a wicked grin on her face, and my heart stopped. "Nice guy!" she yelled before she walked away. I took a deep breath and waited for my heart to start up again. I knew she was just teasing me, but it still freaked me out.

"Want to go out on the porch?" asked Lance when I walked over to him. "It's really hard to talk over the music. And don't worry. I won't take one step off the porch tonight." He held up his hands like he was surrendering.

"Okay, sure," I said. We went outside, but the second we were through the doors I regretted it. Brandon Matheson was out here with a group of Crockett counselors.

I spun around and almost knocked Lance down as he walked up behind me. "Oh, sorry. You know what? I need to get a drink first."

We went back inside and headed for the refreshment

table. Lauren came running up to me. "Hey, this really works! I asked this guy what his favorite video games were, and he's been talking to me all night. And he's a pretty good dancer!" Then she took off to find her dancing gamer.

Well, at least Lauren was having a great night. So far Lance and I hadn't danced even one time. I had to get him to dance to at least a couple of fast songs before I could try to convince him to slow dance.

"Good song, huh?" I yelled at him when a Black Eyed Peas song started up. It was really loud. "I actually like to dance to this song. Do you want to . . .?"

Lance looked at me and shook his head. "Uh, no thanks. I really can't dance at all."

"Oh, I can't either really, but my friend Lauren—you know the one with the blond hair? She showed us a couple of . . ." Just then Mei walked past me with a guy and made a fish-lips face at me.

Lance saw her and laughed. "What's wrong with your friend?"

"She's . . . uh, she has asthma. She makes that face sometimes. I guess it helps her breathe better." Okay, that was the last straw. That girl was getting no more video game info out of me tonight.

"You ready to go outside now?" Lance asked.

That depends. Is Brandon Matheson out there waiting to talk my ear off?

"Are you sure you don't want to dance just one time? Come on. Just one dance." I took his arm and sort of dragged him out on the floor.

"I hate this," Lance groaned. "I'm going to look really stupid."

"Oh, you, me, and fifty other people," I assured him. We were moving to the music when a bunch of people started yelling by the refreshment table.

"What is that all about?" Lance asked, stopping to watch.

"Don't worry about it," I told him, but Lance and everyone around us had all stopped to gawk at Kelly Hedges and Reb Callison screaming their heads off at each other. It was so bad a counselor came and dragged them out.

"Wicked! I love watching girls fight!" said Lance.

Great. Brandon Matheson, gaming consultations, and now a fight. What next? A flood and a couple of plagues?

"Forget about them. Just listen to the music," I told him. Lance did manage to dance with me a little after that, but then he wanted to sit down again.

So we did. And for the next half hour, we didn't

move out of those seats. When the slow songs started, we kept talking. But I didn't have the nerve to ask Lance to get up and dance with me. I knew he didn't really want to. But I wasn't sure if he was embarrassed about slow dancing in general, or if he didn't want to slow dance with *me*. If I were cute like Courtney or little like Mei, then would he have wanted to? Was any boy ever going to like me for myself? If I was JD around my friends, should I be JD around boys, too? Or someone else? And who? Who should I be?

Pretty soon the dance was over, and all the boys were walking out. "Bye, JD! It was fun talking to you," Lance said, right before he walked out of my life forever.

"Bye, see ya later," I told him. But I probably wouldn't. I felt bad for using him at the first dance. All I'd cared about was impressing everyone with how cool I was. But what good did it do making everyone think we'd been kissing when nothing had happened?

Maybe one day I'd get a real kiss from a real boy. Maybe then I wouldn't care what everyone else thought about me. I'd only care what I thought about myself.

CHAPTER 17

Monday, July 7

Hi, everyone!

Thanks for the e-mails. I love getting mail!!! Swim class is going great. We take the final test on Wed. and I'm pretty sure I'll pass. Guess what? I'm going to be in the talent show in three more days! My cabin picked me to be in it. All my friends think I'm really funny. I've ~~got a great~~

~~I'm not sure what I'll do for an act, but it'll be funny.~~

I'm going to fall flat on my face and embarrass myself in front of the whole camp then everyone will find out I'm not funny I'm a fake nobody even knows my

Tell Justin ~~I hate his guts~~ cause he hasn't written me one stinking time all month!! HES NOT THE ONLY ONE WHO HAS PROBLE

I crumpled up the paper and stuck it under my pillow. Then I rolled over so I was facing the wall. Since it was rest hour, I didn't have to talk to anyone. I could just lie on my bunk and act like I was asleep.

I had a headache. And a chest ache. It felt tense and tight, and it had been like that all day. All through breakfast, through swim class, through lunch. The talent show was three days away, and I still had no idea what I was going to do for it.

Then I got two e-mails in my mailbox after lunch, one from Mom and Dad, one from Adam. But nothing from Justin, of course. Why would he bother to write me?

The bell rang, and everyone got up from their bunks and started moving around. I kept my eyes shut and tried to make my face relax.

"Is she asleep?" someone whispered. It sounded like Michelle, but it might've been Amber.

A floorboard creaked and a trunk lid opened, then closed. I heard someone tiptoe over to my bunk. I could feel someone standing by the edge of my bed.

"JD? It's time to go to activities." A hand patted me on the back.

I thought about faking it and acting like I was still asleep, but I didn't want to overdo it. Campers never took naps during rest hour, only counselors. "Naps are my favorite college elective," Michelle had told us once.

I sat up and blinked. Michelle was standing on her tiptoes, looking up at me in my top bunk. "I don't feel well," I said, making my voice sound scratchy. Courtney and Lauren were watching me. Amber sat on her bunk, pulling on her riding boots.

"Are you sick too?" Michelle asked. Meredith had gone to the infirmary yesterday. There was some kind of virus going around.

"I don't know. Maybe." I wanted to get out of afternoon activities, but I also wanted to avoid a trip to the infirmary.

Michelle put her hand on my forehead. "I don't think you have a fever."

I shook my head. "No, I don't have a fever. I just feel so *tired*." I fell back on my bunk and rubbed my eyes.

"We did have a really hard class this morning," murmured Courtney so Alex wouldn't hear her from Side B. "We each had to rescue our partner. Then we swam *eight* laps." It was the most we'd ever had to do.

"Maybe you should take it easy this afternoon," said Michelle.

I nodded and rolled over.

"I hope you feel better," Courtney whispered. I heard Michelle telling Alex I needed to sleep.

When the screen door banged shut for the last time, I kept still and waited to make sure everyone was gone. Then I sat up and looked around. I was so glad to be alone.

I pulled out the crumpled-up paper from under my pillow and tossed it toward the trash can by the door, but I didn't make it. Too bad, or that definitely would've been a three-pointer. I hopped down from my bunk and went to pick up the paper. I wadded it into a really tight ball and tossed it in.

I'd write to them later. Maybe tomorrow, when I felt better. When I wasn't so depressed. And worried.

Justin had a doctor's appt. today. He really is going to pull through all this and be just fine, Mom had written in her e-mail. It sounded like she was trying to convince herself instead of me. Adam didn't even mention Justin. I wondered if they were still fighting with each other all the time, or even worse, not speaking at all. For a long time Justin wouldn't even talk to Adam; he blamed him for what happened.

A whole month at camp was a good break for me, but camp was over on Saturday. Then I'd go back home to . . . everything.

I climbed back up on my top bunk and stretched out. It was sunny outside, but inside the cabin, it was always shady and kind of dark. There was a warm, piney smell coming in through the window screens, and insects were making buzzing noises outside.

My old name tag was lying on the shelf next to my bunk. We hadn't worn these in weeks, because we all knew each other now. I picked it up and looked at it.

JD. The other side was just a dark red smudge where I'd marked it out. I couldn't see the JUDITH at all. But I knew it was there. I held the name tag by the string and flicked the little oval slice of wood with my finger. It spun around. JD. Smudge. JD. Smudge.

What if I'd just been myself? What if I hadn't pretended to be something I wasn't? What would camp have been like for Judith, instead of JD?

"Judith. Judith. Judith Duckworth." It felt funny to say my name out loud. "Judith, how did you manage to screw up your life so much?"

In three more days JD was going to get up onstage and have absolutely nothing to do.

What happened, JD? We thought you were funny.

Sorry, you were wrong. Oh, and by the way, the name's Judith.

I hung my name tag around my neck with the smudge side facing out. That was all I was. A smudge. A nobody.

Then I covered my head with my pillow and started to bawl.

CHAPTER 18

When I heard the screen door open, I wiped my nose. I'd stopped crying by that time, but I was still pretty sniffly. I lay still on my bed, facing the wall. I didn't really want anyone to see me like this.

From the footsteps, I could tell it was Amber. She tried to be quiet, but her riding boots clomped against the wooden floor. So I sat up and looked at her. "It's okay. I'm not really asleep."

Amber's forehead wrinkled up when she saw me. "Are you okay?"

"Yeah." I guess my face was all blotchy from crying.

Amber sat on her bunk and pulled off her boots. "Are you not feeling well, JD?"

I fell back on my bed. "No! I feel awful!" Then I couldn't help it. I started to cry again.

"Is there anything I can get you? Want me to walk you down to the infirmary?" she asked softly.

"No. I'm not sick. I'm just . . . having a bad day." I needed a Kleenex. Michelle had a box beside her bed and I sat up and looked at them. Amber was a mind reader. She went over and pulled one out of the box and brought it to me.

"Thanks, Amber." She was such a sweet girl, but our little Guard Start clique was always together, and nobody from our cabin ever hung out with her much. I knew she had friends—horsey friends. All the girls who took riding lessons were a clique of their own. But maybe Amber and I could've been close friends, if I hadn't overlooked her.

"You're the nicest girl in the cabin," I said.

Amber rolled her eyes and smiled a little. "Oh, please."

"You are. Katherine's the meanest, Isabel's the quietest, Meredith's the fairest, Mei's the feistiest. . . ."

"You're the funniest!"

"No, I'm not!" I sobbed. I was crying my eyes out. It was like the pipes had burst. All the water was gushing out, and I couldn't do anything to stop it. The Kleenex was a shredded piece of fluff. Amber ran and got me a handful.

"I am not funny," I said again. I blew my nose three times. I hadn't cried this hard since I was a little kid. Now I even had the hiccups.

"How can you say that? You are so funny. You're one of the funniest people I've ever met!" She smiled at me. I could tell she really meant it too; she wasn't just trying to cheer me up.

"Amber, I'm . . . I have a secret. I've got to tell someone. If I don't, I think I'm going to explode." I held my breath, trying to make the hiccups stop.

Amber's eyes widened. "Okay."

"I'm . . . all summer I've been trying to be . . . I'm really nothing like everybody thinks I am. That's not the real me. I know I'm always cracking jokes and being a big goof and a real loudmouth." I took a deep breath. It was so stupid that I kept hiccuping. "But before camp, I was *nothing* like that. I was always pretty quiet. I always followed the rules. I was more like"—I started to say *more like you*, but then I stopped myself—"more like Isabel."

Amber's mouth twitched in a half smile. "You were like Isabel?"

"I was! Only maybe not as shy. I was *boring*. Nobody ever noticed me."

"Well, you're not like that now!"

I slid off my top bunk and went over to the mirror. I looked terrible. My eyes were all puffy and red. My face was blotchy. I turned and looked at Amber. "This is just an act! I'm not even JD. That's not my name. Before camp, nobody ever called me that."

Amber frowned. "Did they call you Josephina?"

"No!" I couldn't help laughing. She'd remembered that stupid made-up name from the first day. "I made that up too. My real name is Judith. That's what my family calls me, my friends back home, all my teachers— Judith. Not JD." I crossed my arms and looked at her. There. I'd said it. I'd finally told somebody the truth.

Amber stared back at me. She shrugged a little. "Well, okay. Is that the big secret?"

"Yes! Don't you think it's terrible that I've been pretending to be something I'm not? That I even lied about my name? That nobody at this camp really knows me?"

Amber frowned again. "What have you been pretending to be that you're not?"

"Funny!" I huffed. I threw up my hands. "Crazy! Wacky! A troublemaker! I'm not really like that. Don't you get it?"

Amber raised her eyebrows. "Oh, I get what you're saying. I just . . . don't know what the big deal is. You are funny, JD. You *are*. And so nobody's ever called you JD till now. So what? You're JD to us."

I sat down on the edge of her bed. "But it's a lie. All summer I've just been pretending."

"Maybe that's how it started out. Maybe you were putting on a big act in the beginning, but don't you think you're JD now?" Amber asked.

I stared at a patch of sunlight on the floor. "I don't know." I didn't tell her about trying to be like Chloe Carlson. Now it sounded really silly that I'd wanted to borrow someone else's personality for the summer. "I'm not sure who I am. I'm not really Judith anymore. But JD's just an act. I'm . . ." I started to say "Smudge" because that's who I felt like. A rubbed-out nobody. But that was so ridiculous I started to laugh. I still had the stupid name tag around my neck with the smudge side showing. I took it off and tossed it up to my top bunk.

Amber smiled while I sat there on her bed and giggled. One second I was bawling my eyes out, and now I couldn't stop laughing. Couldn't she see what a mess I was? I finally got ahold of myself.

"And now I'm supposed to do something for the talent show, and I'm going to bomb! I've got to come up with some kind of funny act, but I can't think of anything!"

"You won't bomb. You'll be great."

"Amber! Haven't you heard a word I've said? Do you know how hard I try to come up with funny things to say? It's not like they just pop into my head. I sit there and strain my brain. It's like trying to remember all the state capitals. And then sometimes I can't think of anything funny, and Courtney or Lauren will look at me and say, 'What's wrong with you? You're being so quiet.'"

Amber reached over and patted my leg, because I'd practically been shouting at her. "But it works. You do come up with funny things to say. A lot. You may think that you're not naturally funny, but you really are when you try."

I closed my eyes and leaned my head against the metal bed frame. "What am I going to do for the talent show? I have to get out of it."

"Maybe I can help you."

I opened my eyes and looked at her. "Will you do an act with me?"

"Well, I'll help you think of something to do. You're the actor, remember?"

"Okay, if you can come up with something funny for me to do, I'll do it. I don't mind being up on stage and making a fool of myself, as long as I get laughs. Can you write me a funny poem or something?"

"Funny poem," said Amber slowly, giving it some thought. "What about a song?"

"Yes! Anything!"

Amber bit her lip and smiled. "I need some paper. What if we . . . yeah, you should definitely do a funny song. I'll write the words and you can sing it." She grabbed a spiral notebook and a pen from the shelf by her bed.

"Can I read some of your poems?" I asked.

"Oh, they're not funny. Maybe sometime. Yeah, maybe later. But let's work on this for now."

"Amber, I just want you to know that you are saving my life!" I told her. I let out a huge sigh. For the first time in days I felt like maybe this would all work out.

Amber had a look on her face like the wheels were already starting to turn. "What if we wrote a song kind of like . . ."

The screen door banged open, and the entire Guard Start class walked in. Even Claudia and Shelby.

"Hey! Are you feeling better?" asked Mei.

"We've got great news!" Courtney said.

"What?" The only great news I could think of was that Alex had canceled class for tomorrow.

Courtney was all smiles. "Lauren thought of a great idea for the talent show. We're all going to do a hip-hop routine, and she'll choreograph it for us!"

The whole Guard Start class stood there with huge smiles on their faces, and Amber and I looked at them.

"Well?" asked Courtney when I didn't say anything.

"You've been whining for days about how you needed some help thinking up an act," said Lauren.

"This way you don't have to do it alone. We'll all do it together," added Shelby.

"I'm not much of a dancer, but they talked me into it," Claudia said. "It'll be fun."

"And I have *the* most amazing routine for us to do," said Lauren. "It's one that my sister's high school spirit line did. It had people talking!"

"Why?" I asked.

"Because of the moves. And the music. You have to see it. It's really wild."

"I can't dance," I said. Amber clutched the spiral notebook to her chest. She had a polite little smile on her face, like this was the first time she'd heard anything about a talent show.

"I'll teach you. Don't worry. We've got three days to work on it. We'll practice every spare minute we have." Lauren did a couple of spins across the floor.

"That's a great idea, you guys!" said Amber. She tucked the spiral notebook back on her shelf.

"No, it isn't," I said.

Lauren stopped spinning. Everyone stared at me.

"I mean, yeah, it is a good idea, but Amber was going to help me think of an act too."

"Oh," said Courtney.

"Okay," said Mei. Everyone looked at Amber. Nobody said anything.

"Oh, no, we were just . . . we hadn't really thought of anything to do yet," stammered Amber. "You all do the dance routine. Can I watch you practice?"

"Sure," said Lauren, standing in the middle of the floor with her arms crossed. There was a really long pause while we all looked around at each other.

"So . . . what do you want to do, JD?" Courtney asked.

JD. I was JD again, like I'd always been. Why did I pick Amber, who I barely knew, to spill my guts to? What if I'd picked Katherine instead? Then there'd be a giant banner hanging from the dining hall: JD IS A FAKE! LET'S ALL HATE HER NOW!

"I don't know," I said.

"Well, I think you should do the dance routine," Amber told me. "Honestly, JD. I said I'd help you, but I really didn't have any ideas. And Lauren already has something planned out." Amber smiled at me, that sweet smile. I bet it sucked being the nicest person in the cabin sometimes.

"Whatever," I said.

"Well, we don't want to force you to do it," Lauren said, barely keeping the sarcasm out of her voice. "Do something else. I was only trying to help you out." She kept her arms crossed and watched her toes wiggling in her flip-flops.

I wanted to tell everyone the truth. Just get everything out in the open once and for all. Maybe I'd even tell them all about Justin, too. Then I wouldn't have any more secrets and I could stop all this pretending. I could be me again. Whoever that was.

But Amber had barely blinked when I told her. Was it really such a big deal after all?

"Thanks, you guys. I really appreciate it. Let's do it! This way I won't be by myself. But let me warn you—I dance like a gorilla."

Lauren looked up at me and smiled. "You won't when I'm through with you!"

Tuesday, July 8

"Okay, Claudia and JD, you're both still a little late on that part. Let's break it down." Lauren lined up Claudia and me beside her and showed us one more time. "Now with the music." She nodded at Amber, sitting on the floor next to the iPod speakers. Amber started the music again.

Claudia and I followed along with Lauren while the others watched us.

"Bounce, bounce, together left, together right, shoulders and foot," Lauren called out over the music. She signaled for Amber to stop the music. "Much better. Claudia, you were right on the beat that time, and JD, you just need to pick up the tempo a little more."

I wiped my sweaty face on my shirt. I had no idea

that dancing was such a workout. "Are you sure you don't want to slap a gorilla suit on me and let me prance around while the rest of you do the real dancing?" I asked.

"You're getting it. I can't believe what a good job all of you are doing, considering how little time we've had. Okay, let's take a short break."

We all collapsed on the floor or found seats on one of the wooden benches. We had the whole lodge to ourselves since it was morning free time. A nice breeze blew in from the open doors and windows and cooled us off a little.

"I was wondering," Shelby started off, "if maybe we should tone this down a little?"

Lauren wiped her face with a hand towel. "What do you mean?"

"Well, this dance. It's pretty—extreme. Don't you think maybe it's a little much for the camp talent show?" asked Shelby from where she sat on the floor.

"That's why we're doing it," said Lauren. "It'll be the talk of the night!"

There was no doubt about that. When Lauren had shown us the dance routine she'd planned, we'd all watched her openmouthed. Some of the moves were . . . well, shocking. Just the way we were supposed to shake and move and strut. We even had to do this one part where we totally stuck out our hips. It was hard for me not to laugh every time we did that, because I felt so embarrassed about it.

"When my sister's spirit line did this for the first time, the crowd went wild. The guys, especially. They were all whistling and howling," Lauren had told us.

We'd all agreed we could see why. Lauren had said that some parents had complained about how "mature" the routine was.

"What time is it, Claudia?" asked Lauren.

Claudia looked at her watch. "Ten after one."

"Okay, we've got another twenty minutes till lunch. Let's run through it a few more times. On your feet, ladies!" She jumped up and clapped to get us all motivated.

We all got to our feet and took our places in the two lines Lauren had put us in. At least she'd had enough sense to stick me in the back. "Heads up, eyes forward, backs straight! Music!" Lauren yelled, and Amber turned on Lauren's iPod again so the music came blaring out of the little white speakers.

We did the whole routine from start to finish without Lauren making us stop at all. I did my best to keep up with everyone and not stomp around like a defensive lineman. Amber sat on the floor, hugging her knees and watching us.

"Okay, good! Very good! Much better," said Lauren. "Now let's work on the body roll." She stood with her back to us, talking over her shoulder. "Foot, knee, hips, stomach, chest, then knees in, knees out," she directed, demonstrating the roll for us as she talked. "And remember, when you get to the chest pop, really hit it hard. Pop! Like that."

Amber started the music again, and we all worked on the body roll. When we did the left spin, I saw Alex standing in the open doorway, watching our every move. Oh, great, just what we needed right now—an audience. But I had to get used to the idea. Alex was only one person; in two nights we'd be performing in front of the entire camp.

When the song ended, Amber paused the iPod, and Alex strolled into the lodge. "Excuse me. What do you think you're doing?"

"Practicing for the talent show. Michelle told us we could use the lodge when nobody was down here," said Lauren, lifting up her blond ponytail so she could drape the towel around her neck. Michelle and Meredith had both left this morning for the canoeing honor trip—the reward that all the canoers got for working so hard this summer.

Alex stood in front of us with her arms crossed. "Oh, the problem isn't *where* you're practicing; it's *what* you're practicing."

Lauren shrugged. "A dance. What's the big deal?"

Alex looked at all of us. "The big deal is the type of dance you're doing. Don't you think it's inappropriate?"

"In what way?" Lauren asked innocently. I was so glad to let her do all the talking. I'd had enough run-ins with Alex to last me the whole month. The rest of us kept quiet, watching the two of them.

Alex frowned at us. "It's . . . it's way too edgy. Where'd you even learn dance moves like that?"

"My sister's spirit line did this same routine. It happened to be a huge hit at her high school," said Lauren, conveniently leaving out the part about the parents who'd complained about it. Courtney and I exchanged quick looks. Mei watched a granddaddy longlegs scurry across the wood floor.

"Uh-huh," Alex said. "Well, it's one thing for girls who are sixteen and seventeen to perform those moves. But you guys are only twelve years old."

"Oh, please!" Lauren protested. "We're not babies."

"What if we changed some things? Cleaned it up a little?" asked Courtney.

Alex shook her head. "No. Even that wouldn't help. Nothing about this routine is okay."

"Why? What's so bad about it?" asked Lauren.

"Do you really want to perform dance moves like this in front of Eda? I mean, think about it. What if your parents were in the audience? Wouldn't you be embarrassed to be dancing like that in front of them? And may I remind you that there will be Juniors watching you, and they're only eight and nine years old? Do you think you're setting a good example for them?"

"Alex, please. We just want to do a really cool dance routine. We're not trying to set an example or anything," said Lauren.

"I don't want you guys performing this act. You can do a dance routine, but not using any of those moves! Got it?" She gave us all the death-ray glare.

Lauren nodded but didn't say anything. Alex slowly looked us all up and down one more time before she walked out of the lodge. We all sat there, frozen. We didn't want to speak until we were sure she was gone.

Mei tiptoed over to the open door and checked to make sure the coast was clear.

"I can't believe it!" huffed Lauren. "If only she hadn't seen us."

"What should we do now?" Shelby asked. We all looked at each other.

"I guess we'll have to figure out a new act," I said. "We still have a couple of days. We can come up with something." I glanced at Amber sitting by the iPod speakers, and she gave me a little smile.

Lauren glared at me. "Do I know you? Since when do you listen to Alex?" Everyone else was looking at me too.

"Oh, come on, you guys. You know how much trouble I got into with her. She kicked me out of class once already."

"Yeah, but that was class. This is the talent show. It's not the same. I can't believe you of all people would care about what Alex says," Lauren retorted.

I didn't say anything at first. Everyone waited for me to respond. "Maybe I'm tired of being the rule breaker." I wasn't that crazy about doing the dance in the first place. Alex telling us not to do it seemed like a good way for us all to get out of it.

"Oh, great timing! Now all of a sudden you're gonna be the good little girl and not do this dance because Alex says it's too . . . 'edgy.'" Lauren put air quotes around that last word and rolled her eyes in disgust.

"Hey, she's got a point, JD," said Courtney. "All

summer you've been the rebel, and we've watched Alex yell at you. Yes, she did kick you out of class, but then she let you back in. And anyway, class will be over by the night of the talent show."

"True. If we do the dance, what's the worst she can do to us?" asked Lauren, looking right at me. How many times had I made that same comment? Now it was coming back to haunt me.

"She'll be mad," Shelby said.

"And none of us has ever seen Alex mad before, so won't that be a shocker!" Mei put in.

"We can clean it up a little. Then we can say that we did listen to her," suggested Courtney.

"I just don't want the rest of you to get in trouble," I said. My gosh, what was happening here? I'd started a revolution! Maybe next they'd want to overthrow Eda and take over the whole camp.

"Don't worry about us," Courtney said excitedly. "I've never been a rebel before. Come on, guys. Let's do it! This is our chance to make a big name for ourselves. Imagine the reaction we'll get!"

Lauren nodded with satisfaction. "Now you're talking!"

Claudia smiled. "It might be kinda fun. Our way of getting back at Alex for being so strict with us all summer. It's just dancing. It's not like we're letting anyone drown if we don't listen to her this time."

Shelby kept quiet. Amber sat by the iPod speakers, listening to all of us.

"What do you say, JD?" asked Lauren. "Are you in or out?"

Everyone turned and looked at me. I'd created monsters. Five rebellious, rule-breaking monsters.

I didn't want to do the dance. I wanted to tell them to go ahead and do it without me. But I'd gotten them all into this. I couldn't abandon them now. If they were going to get into trouble, I had to be in there with them.

I forced my mouth into a smile. "Like I always say—rules were made to be broken."

CHAPTER 21

Wednesday, July 9

"Before we get started, I want to congratulate all of you on your hard work. You were all good swimmers to start with, but now you're well on your way to becoming lifeguards." Alex kept talking, telling us how proud she was for all the time we'd put into the class. We sat quietly and listened. What would she be saying about us tomorrow night after the talent show?

The five of us sat lined up on the dock. Lauren had also come down to cheer us on—she was sitting over by the edge of the lake. Now that she was busy choreographing our dance, she didn't seem to mind dropping out of the Guard Start class. "Instead of being a lifeguard when I'm a teenager, I can spend my summers teaching dance," she'd told us. When Courtney had said she could do both if she kept working at it, Lauren had shrugged. "Maybe." She seemed happy with who she was. *Dancer*. It said so right on her shorts. I wondered what my shorts should say.

"Okay, let's start with treading water," Alex announced. We all stood up to dive in. At least it was a nice, sunny morning so the water didn't feel quite so cold.

Once we were all in, Alex timed us with her watch. We only had to tread water for two minutes, but we couldn't use our hands, so that made it a little harder. Still, this part was the easiest. Alex blew her whistle when the time was up.

"Great. Now the weight retrieval," she said. We all climbed up the ladder and stood dripping at the end of the dock. Alex picked up a ten-pound black block and held it in front of her. "Watch closely, everyone. I want you to see where it goes in." Then, with both hands, she heaved it out into the water. It made a big splash and disappeared. "Who's first?" she asked.

I knew I could do it, and I thought maybe watching me dive down for the weight would make everyone else see that it wasn't that hard. But I didn't want to be a show-off.

Claudia stepped up. "I'll go."

"Okay, great. Dive in."

Claudia dove off the end of the dock while we all waited and watched. After a minute she came up sputtering. "I can't even see it!"

"It's okay. Look around and see where you are and remember where it went in. Take a deep breath and try it again. You can do this," Alex assured her.

Claudia paused while she got her breath. Then she dove under again. This time she came up after a minute or so and announced, "I see it. But I didn't get it yet."

She went under again while we waited. Alex looked at us all. "I got to do this test in a clear blue swimming pool. I'll admit it's much, much harder doing it in a lake. But lifeguards have to train in all kinds of water." She watched for Claudia to surface.

This time when Claudia came up, she had the weight with her. She swam up to the edge of the dock like an otter, with her head above water and her hands below the surface. When she got to the ladder, she hoisted the weight up and dropped it on the dock with a thud. I could see the muscles in her arms trembling as she did it. Then she climbed up the ladder and knelt beside us, gasping for air.

"Don't worry," she panted. "It's . . . not . . ." She didn't even bother to finish her sentence.

"Great work! Okay, go relax for a while," Alex told her, and Claudia stumbled over to sit with Lauren on the rock.

"I'll go next," I offered. I watched while Alex heaved the weight back into the water, and then I sprang off the end of the dock. As I swam deeper, the water temperature changed. I passed from cool water into really cold water deep below the surface. And down here, the visibility was really bad. Claudia had stirred up dirt at the bottom of the lake while she'd groped around for the weight. I couldn't see much of anything. I had to feel around until I found it.

When I felt my fingers touch something smooth, I grabbed it and started kicking toward the surface. But the closer I got, the heavier the weight felt. I was almost up when I felt it slipping out of my hands. My hands flailed around wildly, trying to grip it again, but it was gone.

So I surfaced and took a breath. "I dropped it! I was almost up when it slipped!" I shouted. I was so frustrated that I didn't get it on the first try. I tried to stay right above where I knew the weight had fallen.

"It gets heavier as you get closer to the surface," yelled Alex from the dock.

"I noticed!"

I took long, deep breaths and then did a surface dive

to go under again. This time I didn't worry so much about seeing the weight. Instead I did it mostly by feel. When I had it in my hands again, I crouched on the bottom, then pushed up with my legs as hard as I could, clutching the weight against my midsection. I shot up to the surface a lot faster this time, and I was able to keep a firm grip on the weight. I paddled over to the dock and lifted it up.

"Excellent!" Alex said.

After I got my breath, I told the others what I'd figured out—to feel for it instead of trying to look through the dark, muddy water. And to hold it against your body and use your legs to kick off from the bottom.

"Very good advice," agreed Alex.

Shelby went next, and we were all amazed that she got it on the first try. We cheered like crazy when she came up and plopped the weight on the dock. "That really helped!" Shelby told me with a grin as she climbed up the ladder. "Thanks!"

Mei was next. It took her three times, but finally, on the last try, she had the block in her arms.

After Courtney's turn, Alex asked us if we were ready to swim the five hundred. We had to do a total of ten laps back and forth across the lake. Four laps had to be the crawl, two laps had to be the breaststroke, but the rest could be any combination. This part wasn't timed, but we did have to do all the laps without stopping for very long.

The thing I liked about swimming was that after a while, I'd fall into a rhythm, and then it wouldn't even feel like I was swimming at all. It was almost like walking someplace when you weren't paying attention to where you were going. It took a long time to get tired out when you were walking, and that was how swimming was for me, if I took it slow and steady.

All kinds of thoughts passed through my brain. Sometimes little bits of a song would pop into my head, or I'd remember parts of a conversation. At times I'd count one-two-three-four as I did my strokes. It was almost like being hypnotized. Swimming a bunch of laps always made me feel good. At the end I'd be tired, but it was a good kind of tired.

We'd all started off in a group, but now everyone was spread out. Sometimes I'd feel someone near me, but other times it felt like I had the lake to myself.

When I was on the sixth lap, I switched to the breast-stroke, just to give myself a change of pace. Now, with my head forward when I came up for air, I could see things a little better than when I was turning to the side to breathe on the crawl. I watched as Alex and the dock got closer and closer with every breath.

By the tenth lap, I'd really slowed down, and I switched back to the crawl again. I took long, slow strokes in the water so I could rest as I finished up. When I was within thirty feet of the dock, I let myself glide up, just kicking with my feet. Then I reached the ladder.

Alex gave me her hand as I climbed up. "Congratulations! You've passed," she told me. I looked back to see everyone else still in the water. I felt kind of light-headed, but other than that, I wasn't too tired.

I sat on the rock with Lauren and waited while the others swam their laps. "How does it feel?" she asked me.

"I'm glad it's all over."

One by one, the rest of them finished their laps. "Congratulations!" Alex shouted at each person as she climbed out. She was all smiles, and she looked so proud of us. When the class first started, I'd really thought that Alex was out to get us all—me especially. She'd been so strict, and she never smiled. But now I realized that all along, all she'd cared about was teaching us so that we'd do well in the class.

"That's it! Congratulations, everyone!" Alex whooped and applauded for all of us, and so did Lauren. It was hard to believe that all our hard work was finally behind us.

Alex told us we could go change into dry clothes. For once, we didn't have to stay at the lake after our lesson to do service hours.

"I knew you'd all pass," said Lauren. She looked happy for us. "I hate to say this, but—we have to rehearse after lunch."

We all groaned, because after such an exhausting morning, we weren't looking forward to another workout. But the talent show was tomorrow night. We really needed some more practice.

"Bye, Alex! See you at lunch," I yelled to her as we all walked off wrapped up in our towels. She had really helped us all get through the test—telling us what a good job we were doing and encouraging us through the tough parts.

Today she was our proud teacher. But that might all change by tomorrow night.

Thursday, July 10

"JD, I need to talk to you about something," said Michelle, just as we were all leaving for morning activities.

"Okay," I said, knowing that anytime someone started a conversation like that, it couldn't be good. Courtney, Mei, and Lauren stood by the door waiting for me.

"She'll just be a second," Michelle told them. They all walked out the door, looking at me over their shoulders as they left. Michelle waited to make sure they were gone. Then she sat cross-legged on her cot and patted a spot beside her for me to sit. She gave me her big grin, her eyes crinkling at the edges.

"What are you doing for the talent show tonight?" Michelle had been away for two days on the overnight canoeing trip, so she was out of the loop.

"Oh, I'm doing something with the whole Guard Start class," I said.

"What is it?"

"A hip-hop dance. Lauren taught it to us." I didn't like where this conversation was going.

"Really? Because Alex told me she saw you guys rehearsing. And she said the dance you were doing was totally inappropriate for girls your age." Michelle spoke in a soft voice. It reminded me of my mom reading me a bedtime story when I was four.

"We changed some things, though. She thought some of the moves were too 'edgy,' but we took those parts out," I said, trying to believe what I was saying.

Michelle patted my hand and then held on to it. "JD, listen. I don't want you girls doing anything at the talent show that might be inappropriate."

"But it's just a dance. And Lauren's sister did this same routine with her school's spirit line and the audience loved it," I said. I pretended that Lauren was talking instead of me.

"Fine, but remember that you'll be in front of the whole camp. Eda, all the younger girls—everyone." Michelle looked me right in the eye. "I trust you to have good judgment, JD. You're a real leader for all these girls. They'll listen to you. Please don't do anything that

❤ 188 ❤

would be an embarrassment for anyone." She gave me this really intense look, and I nodded. I wanted to turn away. It was so hard to look at her.

Michelle stood up and gave me a hug. "Okay, that's all. Go find your friends."

I walked out of the cabin with my head spinning. I felt like Michelle had hypnotized me or something. I knew I would do anything she asked me to. I ran down the hill to where the whole Guard Start group was waiting for me.

"What happened?" asked Courtney.

I didn't say anything at first. Michelle's words still bounced around inside my head. *Good judgment. A real leader.*

"Well? What did she want?" Mei asked. "We knew something was up just by the way she sounded."

I looked at all of them. "We can't do the dance."

"What?" cried Lauren. "No way! The talent show is tonight!" I noticed she had her iPod and speakers with her.

"I guess Alex told her about watching us rehearse and how 'inappropriate' it was. So Michelle doesn't want us to do it."

"Wait a second," said Claudia. "Did she specifically say, 'Do not do the dance'?"

"More or less."

"She used those exact words?" Claudia went on.

"She made it very clear that she didn't want us to do anything that might be embarrassing."

"I'm not embarrassed by it," said Lauren. "I think it's an awesome dance."

"Me too," said Courtney. "I don't think it's inappropriate. Or embarrassing."

"Look, you guys. Both of our counselors have pretty much forbidden us to do this act. We really can't go through with it," I said. *They'll listen to you.*

"Yes, we can," Lauren argued. "Aren't rules made to be broken?" She raised her eyebrows and looked at me.

"What's the worst they can do to us?" asked Mei. "Camp is over on Saturday. "What are they going to do—give us detention? Fail us? Send us to the principal's office?"

"Yeah, JD. Why are you so worried about getting in trouble all of a sudden? Doesn't JD stand for 'Juvenile Delinquent'?" Courtney asked.

Why had I made that speech so many times this summer? I just had to brag about what a troublemaker I was.

"Come on. We need to rehearse. I've already asked one of the Senior counselors if we can use their lodge to practice. Just so we don't have anyone snooping around." Lauren turned and walked away. Claudia followed her. Shelby, Mei, and Courtney stayed put.

"Are you coming?" asked Courtney.

"No."

That was the answer I wanted to give. And it wasn't because Michelle and Alex didn't approve. I didn't want to do the dance. For once, I didn't make a decision based on what everyone else might think about me. I made it for myself.

Lauren and Claudia stopped. They turned around and looked at me. All eyes were on me. Nobody said anything. I realized my toes were cold from the dewy grass. I only had on flip-flops. Everyone was waiting for me to say something else.

"I'm not going to do it," I said.

Shelby cleared her throat. "Me neither."

Lauren stood in front of us with her arms crossed. She gave us a long look. Then, slowly, she nodded. "Fine. The four of us will do it without you." She turned away.

"I don't think you should," I said. My arms were crossed too.

"Well, that's your opinion," said Lauren. Then she and Claudia walked off. Mei and Courtney hadn't moved.

"Come on, JD," Courtney begged, her voice just

above a whisper. "Do it with us. If you're part of the act, it won't be such a shocker. Everyone expects something crazy from you."

"Let's do something else," I suggested. "Something they won't get mad at us about."

"It's too late for that," said Mei. "We've worked so hard at this. All of us."

I looked at the grass in front of me. "No. I'm not going to do the dance. And I don't think you guys should either."

There was a long pause. The four of us stood there. Lauren and Claudia were now almost out of sight.

"Well, I'm sorry you feel that way. I still want to do it," said Courtney.

"Me too," said Mei. Then they walked off, leaving Shelby and me standing there.

Shelby pushed her bangs out of her eyes and looked at me. "Think they'll get into big trouble if they go through with it?"

"I don't know. I have no idea what's going to happen," I said.

So much for being a leader everyone would listen to.

Amber—

Hey!! Guess what? This morning Michelle told me she doesn't want us doing the dance. Now Shelby and I aren't doing it, but the rest of them still are. I know it's totally last minute, but I was thinking-maybe I should come up with a different act??!! What do you think? I don't want everyone else to get in trouble. Got any ideas?? I'm desperate!!! See me after rest hour—K? THANKS!!

JD

I folded the piece of paper into a triangle-shaped paper football and took aim. I flicked it toward Amber's bottom bunk, but it missed and landed on the floor. She still saw it, though, so she reached down and picked it up. Lauren gave me a look from her top bunk, but I kept my eyes on Amber, watching her unfold the piece of paper.

When she finished reading it, she looked up at me with wide eyes. "Well?" I mouthed to her. She shrugged her shoulders, then gave me an okay sign with her fingers.

Rest hour had just started, so we all had to lie there on our bunks and be quiet the whole time. Michelle was asleep, as usual, so I might have been able to get down from my bunk and go talk to Amber, but I didn't want to chance it.

I felt pretty rotten that I was asking Amber for help now. We had only a single afternoon to figure something out. Maybe it was too late.

Amber opened her spiral notebook, and I watched her flip through the pages and start writing. She looked up at me and smiled. I let out a sigh. At least she was going to try.

All through rest hour, Amber scribbled away. The only sound in the cabin was her pen scratching across the page.

When the bell rang and rest hour was over, Lauren, Mei, and Courtney left together without saying even one word to me. So had I lost all my friends by making this decision? I guess they felt like I'd abandoned them.

Michelle sat up on her cot and rubbed her eyes. "Come on, you two. Get moving. Time for activities."

I slid off my bunk and looked at Amber. "I am so sorry to put you on the spot like this at the last minute. If you don't think there's enough time, it's okay."

Amber closed her notebook and bit her lip. "Well, I admit it's not going to be easy to pull this together. But you know that day I said I would help you? I already had an idea then. That's what I've been working on during rest hour."

"Great! Amber, thank you so much! So what's your idea?"

"Well, like I said the last time, I think you should do a song. A funny song. I've been working on the lyrics, but I still need help on some parts. But here's the problem. I can't work on this now. I have to go to the stables and watch a friend jump her horse this afternoon. So can I meet you later?" She was already pulling on her riding boots.

"Absolutely," I told her. What a relief that she was even going to try to help me.

"But I need you to do a few things while I'm at the stables. Can you go to Crafts Cabin and get a bunch of brown yarn? As much as they can spare."

"Um, okay," I agreed. "What's it for?"

Amber smiled shyly at me. "I'll tell you later. And then, do you know Jamie Young, the riflery counselor? She's in Cabin Three."

"Oh, yeah. I know her. She's my friend Natasha's counselor."

"Okay, go find Jamie and ask her if you can borrow her Hawaiian shirt. It has parrots on it."

"Yarn and a Hawaiian shirt. Gotcha." These were weird requests, but if Amber had told me to find the horn of a unicorn, I would've done it.

"I'll meet you back in the cabin around four o'clock. We have a ton of work to do, but I think it's a pretty good idea."

"Oh, Amber! Thank you, thank you, thank you!" I left the cabin to go round up the stuff she wanted. I couldn't wait to find out what she had planned for me. Maybe I could knit while I danced the hula. Anything, as long as I had an act to do.

CHAPTER 24

"Are you nervous?" asked Amber.

"A little," I admitted. It was the whole waiting part that was hard. I figured once I was onstage, JD would take over and I could be my crazy self. Or my crazy made-up self.

"You look great," Amber said.

"Thanks! It feels like Halloween." I shook my brown yarn locks. I just hoped my wig would stay on. Amber held the Slinky dog for me.

All the people doing acts were crowded outside the kitchen doors at the back of the dining hall, waiting our turn. Inside, the whole camp was watching as one act after another went onstage. Through the screen windows we could hear a Junior girl playing "Yesterday" on the piano. She was pretty good, considering she was only eight.

Lauren, Mei, Courtney, and Claudia were all waiting out here too, but some Senior girls stood between our two groups. All day I'd barely seen or spoken to my friends. Was this how camp was going to end—with those guys not even talking to me, and with Amber as my new bff? Everything was so mixed up and weird.

"I guess Lauren's group is going through with it," I whispered to Amber.

"I guess so," she whispered back. "Maybe they cleaned it up, like they said they would. Maybe it won't be too outrageous." That was Amber—always looking on the bright side. The group was dressed in matching white shorts and pink tanks. I'd seen them going around to different cabins today, borrowing the clothes they needed.

Then I looked over and saw Mei wiggling through the crowd toward me.

"I'm not going through with it," she announced when she reached me.

"What?" I asked. "How come?"

Mei shrugged and bit her lip. "I just . . . I'm not sure what's going to happen. Michelle and Alex will definitely be mad. What if we really do get into trouble?"

I glanced over at Lauren and the others. The dance group was now down to three. I could see Lauren's furious expression. Courtney was talking to her and gesturing.

"I'm gonna go talk to them," I said, pushing through the crowd to get to them.

"Oh, hi, Benedict. How's it going?" Lauren glared at me as I walked up.

"Hi, guys," I said, ignoring her remark. "If you don't want to do your dance, it's okay. Just let me go on and make a fool of myself, all right? I'll be Cabin Two's act."

"This is all your fault!" snapped Lauren. "The only reason I suggested doing this dance in the first place was to help you out. And then you go and desert us! Now nobody wants to do it!"

"Then let me do it!" I shot back. "You guys can pull out!"

"I don't want to pull out! I want to do the dance! We spent hours and hours working on it." Lauren threw up her hands while Courtney and Claudia stood silently by, looking helpless.

Mei and Amber came over to us. "Lauren, just let it go. JD has something funny planned," Mei told her.

"What a waste! All that time we spent! And for what? Nothing! You're all a bunch of wimps." Lauren pointed at me. "You started this. If you hadn't backed out, none of the others would have."

She was right. It was my fault. If I could've thought of an act on my own, none of this would've happened. And now everything was falling apart.

"Look, let's . . ." Everyone stared at me, waiting for me to say something. There they all were, in their little matching outfits. And they were all good dancers. If only Alex hadn't seen us rehearsing that day. If only Michelle hadn't hypnotized me into being a good girl this morning. Would it be so bad if they did the dance? What was the worst that could happen?

"What if . . . why don't we do them together? I'll do my act onstage, and you guys can all be my backup dancers," I blurted out. It was the only thing I could think of.

"What? We're supposed to go on in about five minutes!" yelled Lauren. "We don't even know what you're doing for an act!" She looked me up and down. I had on Jamie Young's Hawaiian shirt with parrots all over it and three packages of brown yarn hanging on my head. It was supposed to look like long wavy hair.

"I'm singing 'Camp Days,'" I told them. "Amber made up funny lyrics for me. I'm doing a Weird Al imitation," I added, in case they didn't recognize me.

"'Camp Days'?" asked Mei. "'Camp Days! Camp

Days! We frolic and skip in the dew, the dew'? You're singing that song?" Her jaw dropped.

"Yeah! It'll be funny! You guys back me up. Come on! Let's do it!"

"No way!" said Lauren. "No way are we going to go out there and dance to some stupid camp song without any real music! It'll mess up the whole routine!"

"Middler Cabin Two? Where's the act for Middler Cabin Two?" shouted Lydia Duncan, one of the CATs. They were organizing everything, telling people when to go on.

"Over here!" called Amber, waving the Slinky dog over her head.

"You guys are next. I need you over here by the door. As soon as the juggler finishes, you're on."

"No, we can't be next!" Courtney yelled across the crowd to her. "We're not ready!"

"Yes, we are!" I yelled back. Then I turned to the rest of them. "You guys, please! This will work! I'm going out there and I'll sing 'Camp Days' while all of you dance behind me. Can't you imagine how funny that will be?"

"The dance we're doing is *not* funny," Lauren insisted. She had her arms crossed, and she looked like she wasn't going to budge.

I grabbed her shoulders. "Lauren, listen. If you do the

dance the way you practiced it, everyone's gonna freak. But if you do it while I'm singing some ridiculous song, it'll give the whole camp a chance to see your amazing choreography and the group's awesome moves. And no one will get upset about it. Trust me."

Courtney nudged her with her elbow. "It might be a good idea. We all know the dance by heart. We could do it without any music at all."

"I can't believe this is happening," said Lauren, shaking her head.

"Cabin Two! Front and center!" Lydia called.

"Hey, if we're all going on, what about Shelby?" asked Claudia.

Shelby! Oh my God, we'd completely forgotten about her. Since she'd backed out of doing the dance, she was sitting in the audience with all the other campers.

I turned to Amber. "Can you go find her? Tell her what we're doing and get her to dance with us."

"She's not dressed for it," Lauren reminded me.

"We'll figure something out," I said. I pushed my way through all the other girls standing around till I reached the kitchen door where Lydia was waiting.

"Okay, as soon as the applause stops, I'll announce you, and then you guys go on. Does your act have a name?" Lydia asked me.

"Uh, the Dancing Fools," I told her, saying the first thing that came to mind. The others had joined me, and we were all outside the door.

"We can't go on now," said Claudia. "What about Shelby?"

"I'm not going on at all," Lauren insisted. "I'm not a dancing fool."

"We need a few more minutes," I told Lydia. "Can you send someone else on next?" I begged her.

"We'll go," said a couple of Senior girls standing behind us, dressed in togas.

"Fine. As long as the show goes on," Lydia said, disappearing with them through the screen door.

Just then Michelle appeared with a can of Coke. "Amber told me you might need this," she said. "Drink up."

"Oh, yes! You're a lifesaver." I grabbed the can and took three big gulps. Amber had remembered to ask Michelle to buy me a drink from the counselors' vending machine.

"Hey, where's our liquid refreshment?" asked Mei with her hands on her hips.

"Do you need to burp too?" Michelle asked.

"What are you talking about?" cried Mei.

"No, you don't need to burp! Just dance!" I told her before taking two more swigs.

Amber came dashing up with Shelby. "I found her!"

"Shelby, you're all dancing behind me while I sing," I said in between swallows of Coke. The pressure was starting to rise.

"She's not dressed!" Lauren protested.

Shelby had on a gray Pine Haven sweatshirt and denim shorts. "Stick her in the middle. It'll be fine," said Mei.

Lydia came out of the kitchen door. "Dancing Fools, are you ready now? Because you're next." Inside, we could hear the applause for the last act.

"We're ready!" I said, handing Michelle the empty can. I was about to explode.

"Wait! Your dog!" yelled Amber, tossing me the Slinky dog. It had a stuffed head and backside, but its middle looked like a plastic accordion.

I followed Lydia through the kitchen to the swinging door that led to the dining room. Through the door I could hear the sound of a couple hundred people shuffling around in seats and making noise. The rest of the girls crowded up behind me.

Lydia went through the door and announced, "And now, from Middler Cabin Two, please welcome The Dancing Fools."

Everyone applauded as I rushed out on the stage. It

was just a wooden platform at one end of the dining hall. All the tables had been moved out, and the audience was sitting in long rows of chairs.

There was only one problem. I was all alone. I could see Courtney peek through the swinging door, and the others were standing behind her, still arguing. Or at least it looked that way. Were they not going to follow me? Should I go ahead and start singing without them? There was a long pause while I stood there, clutching the Slinky dog and looking at the door. I could hear a couple of snickers.

Then Courtney, Mei, and Claudia came running out. They got more applause, but it was pretty obvious that none of us knew what to do. Mei kept motioning to Lauren and Shelby while we all looked at the door. Again I heard some laughter.

"We really did rehearse this!" I said loudly. I got several laughs, and then the door swung open and Lauren and Shelby ran out. Lauren's face was beet red, but I doubted anyone in the audience could see it. They all lined up the way we'd done in rehearsals. Shelby stood in the middle in her Pine Haven sweatshirt, and with two girls in pink tanks on either side of her, it looked like we'd planned it that way.

I took a deep breath and walked to the edge of the

platform. "Tonight we'll be performing a lovely camp tune you're all familiar with. It's called 'Camp Days.'" I made loud throat-clearing noises and held up the dog like an accordion. I heard Lauren count off in a whisper, and the girls began to dance as I sang to the tune of "My Bonnie Lies Over the Ocean."

Pine Haven, I try to forget you.
Your meals give me gas all night long.

I let out the huge burp that had been building up inside me. A roar of laughter exploded across the dining hall.

Your lake makes me freeze all my toes off.
Tadpoles in my suit—that's just wrong!

By now I had to shout over all the noise of people laughing. I pumped the dog's belly like an accordion while my backup dancers strutted behind me.

Camp Days! Camp Days! We frolic and skip in the
dew, the dew!
Camp Days! Camp Days! We frolic and skip in the
dew!

Mosquitoes and gnats have attacked me.
A spider laid eggs in my bed.
I think there's a bear up in that tree.
The frog in my trunk might be dead.
Camp Days! Camp Days! We frolic and skip in the
dew, the dew!
Camp Days! Camp Days! We frolic and skip in the
dew!
Pine Haven, we're trapped here all summer.
I want to take showers alone.
This camp life is really a bummer.
Oh, Eda! We want to go home!

The wild moves that Lauren had taught everyone now looked really funny with me singing this ridiculous song. Nobody could be offended by the dancing now.

I realized that the group was only partway through their dance, so I started again at the beginning, pumping the accordion dog like crazy. When I got to the line about tadpoles in my swimsuit, I wriggled and jumped around. The whole dining hall was going wild. I'd never had such a big response.

When I got to the last verse, the dancers had stopped, and they stepped forward on either side of me.

We all sang the last lines, *"Oh, Eda! We want to go home!"* together.

By that time, people weren't just applauding; they were stomping their feet and cheering. We took our bows and then ran back through the swinging door.

Amber was waiting for us on the other side. "That was awesome! It was amazing! It looked like you'd rehearsed it for weeks!"

We all slumped over on the stainless steel sinks and countertops around the kitchen. I couldn't believe we'd done it. It was over, and it'd been huge.

Lauren wiped beads of sweat off her forehead. "Good job, everyone." Then she looked at me and burst out laughing. "The crowd loved it! We're Dancing Fools!"

Friday, July 11

"Mei Delaney, JD Duckworth, Claudia Ogilvie, Shelby Parsons, and Courtney Prosser." Alex read off our names, and everyone clapped politely as we went up to get our certificates.

She shook hands with each of us as she handed out the pieces of paper—one was a Red Cross certificate that said we'd passed the Guard Start class, and the other was a Pine Haven certificate that read, "In Recognition of Special Accomplishments in Swimming."

We were about to sit down when Alex stopped us. "I'd also like to recognize Lauren Haigler for her accomplishments in swimming this summer. Lauren completed thirty service hours, and she was a great help and inspiration in our swimming program."

Alex motioned Lauren to come up and join us. I could see that half-annoyed, half-embarrassed look Lauren always got whenever people complimented her, but she came up beside us, shook hands with Alex, and accepted the Pine Haven certificate.

We all sat down and took our places while the awards assembly went on. Since tomorrow was the last day, we were having a special Friday assembly on the hill.

I sat by my friends and clapped for other people as they received different certificates. Meredith got one for canoeing, and Isabel got one from Libby Sheppard for learning how to swim this summer. Some people got awards for tennis, and some got them for hiking and rappelling. I felt a little bummed that I'd never gotten around to doing all the activities I'd wanted to this summer.

But I was glad I'd finished the Guard Start class. Not only finished, I was the best swimmer in the class—Alex had said so herself. That was a great feeling—knowing that I was really, really good at something. My family would be so proud of me. I still hadn't decided if I ever wanted to be a lifeguard, but finishing the class made me feel like I'd accomplished something all on my own that had nothing to do with being JD.

When the counselors finished giving out certificates

for activities, Eda had a few awards of her own. She announced the winners for the talent show, and the Dancing Fools all had to go up and receive certificates for getting second place.

When they had announced the winners last night at the end of the talent show, we had all screamed our lungs out. We'd been happy just to get through it; it had never even occurred to us that we might come close to winning.

Everyone cheered and hooted as Eda handed us our certificates. When the applause died down, I said, "The Dancing Fools want to thank Amber Cummings for writing such great lyrics! Amber, come up here!"

Amber was sitting in the grass beside Michelle and Alex, and she covered her face with her hands when I mentioned her name. But Michelle nudged her, and Amber came up and joined us. "We never could've done it without Amber!" I yelled over the applause. And that was true. She'd come through for all of us.

We all sat down again and listened as other awards were given out. It'd been so much fun working on the song with Amber. I couldn't believe what a great idea she'd come up with. Basically, she'd written all the lyrics during rest hour yesterday, which amazed me. I only added a few things: the part about freezing in the lake and getting tadpoles stuck in your swimsuit. And Amber had written the last line as "Oh, Mommy, we want to come home!" but I thought about Shelby and the way she'd felt when I'd made that stupid mommy joke. So I'd suggested changing the line to "Oh, Eda! We want to go home!" and Amber had agreed to it.

Now people were saying that from now on, everyone at camp would sing our version of "Camp Days" instead of the sappy original. We all thought that was pretty cool. And everyone had raved about how good the dancers were, and how funny it was to mix those moves with that goofy song.

"Now we'll go ahead with regularly scheduled activities today. Then tonight we will have the final Circle Fire," announced Eda.

Meredith stopped us as the crowd stood up and started walking away. "Hey, guys, it really was a great act. But why'd you keep the chorus the same as the original?"

"Are you kidding me? How could we improve on frolicking and skipping in the dew?" I asked.

Then Michelle walked up. "I am so proud of all my campers! You guys did a great job." Then she grabbed my arm and pulled me aside. "Thank you," she whispered.

"For what?" I asked.

"For taking care of things. For making sure that your act was appropriate." She smiled at me. Courtney and everyone else wandered away while Michelle and I talked.

"Believe me—it all came together at the last minute," I told her.

"Well, however it happened, I'm glad it worked out. I can't believe camp is over tomorrow!" Michelle groaned.

"I know," I agreed. "I don't want to leave. I wish I could stay here forever. I love this place."

"Oh, come on. Camp is great, and we're all going to be sad saying good-bye, but look at the bright side. You'll be so happy to see your family tomorrow."

"Yeah, I will be," I said. Then I looked at her. "But my family's a mess." If there was anyone I could tell this secret to, it was Michelle.

Her eyebrows went up, and she waited for me to go on. I'd never talked about this to anyone.

"We're having a lot of problems now. I'm glad I've been away all summer. In some ways I don't want to go home." I looked at her. "Do you think that's terrible?"

"No, of course not," said Michelle. A little line appeared between her eyes. "Do you want to talk about it?"

"Yeah, I think so. But not here." A lot of people were still wandering around after the assembly.

Michelle nodded. "Let's go someplace private."

So we went to Middler Lodge and sat out on the porch. The view was beautiful from up here, with the blue mountains off in the distance. And today was a sunny day.

Michelle kept quiet and waited for me to talk. I was glad we were sitting on a wooden bench looking out at the view. That way I didn't have to look at her.

"Well, you know all about my brothers and how they're big football heroes?" I asked. Michelle nodded. "That's how it used to be. But it's not that way anymore. Not since this spring."

Michelle looked concerned. "Did one of them get injured?"

"No," I said. Injuries they could recover from. "No. It was Justin. He got caught using steroids."

"Oh," said Michelle very quietly.

"Yeah. And guess who turned him in."

"The coach?" she asked.

"No. Adam told on him. He went to the coaches and told them first, before he even told my parents about it. It was a huge scandal. Everybody in the school knew about it. It was in the newspaper. We live in kind of a small town, and during the fall everything revolves around Friday night football. The whole town was talking about the Duckworth brothers and what happened at Central High."

Michelle blew a long breath out. "I can imagine. It must have been terrible."

"It was. Everybody took sides. Some people said the coaches knew about it but looked the other way. A lot of people were mad at Adam for telling on Justin. Adam said he did it because he was afraid Justin might have bad side effects from the drugs. But then Justin said Adam only narced on him because he was jealous. You know, Justin's older and stronger and bigger. I think maybe Adam was a little jealous."

"Well, for whatever reason he did it, Adam did the right thing," said Michelle, glancing at me. "Steroids can cause so many health problems. It was dangerous for Justin to be on them. You know that, right?"

"Yeah, I do. But it's messed up our whole family. People have broken windows in our house—they drive by at night and throw rocks. And one time when I was walking home from school, a reporter jumped out from behind a bush and asked me if I knew my brother was 'on the juice.'" I tried to tell that part without crying.

Michelle put her arm around me and patted my

shoulder. Now I really felt like crying. "So that's why I'm not looking forward to going home. Sure, I love them and miss them. But I don't want to go home to all that. My parents sent me to camp so I could get away from everything."

I felt like I'd just run a mile. I was so exhausted and relieved. I took long, deep breaths. I actually did feel better, now that I'd finally told someone my big secret.

"Well, it can't be easy," Michelle said. I could tell she was trying to think of the right words. "Things will get better over time. How's your brother doing now?"

I shrugged. "It's hard to say. He hasn't written me all summer. He's been pretty withdrawn from our whole family. I think he's depressed. We're not sure if he'll be allowed to play football next year. But that's all he cares about. If he's not a football player, he doesn't know"—I stopped talking because I realized Justin and I had something in common—"he doesn't know who is."

For most of his life Justin had been a football player. He'd played since he was a little boy, starting out in Pop Warner. It was like Lauren having "Dancer" on her shorts. Justin wore his jersey and that was who he was. But now what?

"It's a tough lesson for him," Michelle admitted. "Hopefully, he'll be able to move on and get his life back on track."

I nodded. Then I started crying. I felt guilty for saying I didn't want to go home. What would my family think if they heard that? But I dreaded having to go back and face everything. There was nothing I could do, though. I couldn't stay at camp forever.

Michelle kept quiet and patted me on the shoulder till I calmed down. My nose was runny, but I didn't have anything to blow it on. Michelle stuck out her arm and offered me her sleeve, which made me start laughing. "Go ahead! I can always wash this shirt later!" she said cheerfully.

"I am not going to blow my runny nose on your shirt!" Now I couldn't stop laughing.

"Want me to pull some leaves off the trees, then?" she asked, looking up at some tree branches just a few feet away from the porch.

"NO! I'll just sniffle." I took a deep breath. I really did feel better. "Thanks, Michelle."

She looked at me and smiled a little. "Are you sure you're okay now?"

"Yeah. I really am." We got up and left the porch. I went to Solitary and washed my face before anyone could see me.

Everyone was waiting for me in the cabin. "Where'd you go?" asked Courtney.

"I was talking to Michelle about something," I told her. Nobody said anything about my face, so I figured all the crying signs were gone.

"So what activity should we go to this morning?" Lauren asked. "Since nobody has to go to the lake and swim laps."

"How about tennis?" I suggested. They all thought that was a weird choice, since we'd barely played all summer, but they agreed to go with me.

The four of us walked out of the cabin swinging our tennis rackets. "Would you guys have liked me if I wasn't always cracking jokes and getting into trouble?" I asked suddenly.

"Of course," said Mei. "But it's hard to imagine you not doing those things."

"What if I said that before I came to camp, I had a completely different personality?"

"What if I said that my biological parents were from outer space, and they sent me to this planet because our home planet was about to be destroyed? And here on Earth, I have special powers," said Mei.

"Like what?" asked Courtney.

"I can do this!" Then Mei started doing all the steps from the dance routine, which made Courtney and Lauren crack up.

"Hey, you stole *my* special powers!" Lauren yelled, and bumped Mei out of the way with her hip so she could do the dance.

"I'm trying to tell you guys something!" I cried. They all stopped and looked at me. "If you'd met me before camp, you wouldn't even recognize me."

"Why? Did you used to be four-six instead of five-six?" asked Courtney.

"No. I just act very different at home than I do here. That's all."

Lauren shrugged. "Well, we all do."

"Do any of you even know that my real name is Judith?" I asked.

"Judith?" Mei covered her mouth with her hand and snickered. "*Judith?* I've never heard that one before!"

"Well, it is," I said firmly. "And I want you all to start calling me that."

They burst out laughing. "Okay, Judith. Whatever you say," Mei agreed.

Not one of them even acted surprised. They didn't seem to get what I'd just told them. "I'm not joking about this, you guys! At home I'm this quiet, boring girl named Judith Duckworth. But when I came to camp I decided to change that, and so I told everyone to call me JD. But I'm not JD. I'm Judith.

Tomorrow we all go home, and I have to go back to being myself."

Lauren pretended to smack my back with the tennis racket. "Look, JD—or Judith. Or John Jacob Jingleheimer Schmidt. We're your friends, no matter what we call you."

"Yeah, but . . ." How could I explain it so they'd understand?

Courtney solemnly put her hand on my forehead. "Do you feel okay, Schmitty?"

"Problem solved! Let's call her Schmitty from now on!" said Mei.

I felt pretty silly. Maybe my whole personality makeover wasn't such a big deal after all. They didn't even care! "Stop calling me Schmitty! Call me . . . whatever. I guess it doesn't matter."

Courtney shook her head and whispered to Mei and Lauren, "I'm really worried about Schmitty. She's not herself today."

"I am myself! I think. Let's just go play tennis and have fun, okay? It's our last full day together."

I did feel like myself. And maybe Lauren was right. Maybe it didn't matter what they called me. Whatever name I went by, somehow I would manage to be me.

CHAPTER 26

Saturday, July 12

I hated the way the cabin looked exactly like it had on the first day we got here. All the mattresses were bare, and everybody's stuff was packed away. That day I'd been so excited. Now I was just depressed.

But I had one last thing to do in the cabin before leaving. I took a pen out of my backpack and climbed up on my top bunk. It didn't seem like my bed anymore, because now my sheets and blanket were packed. I found the spot on the wall where I'd written JD WAS HERE. Under it, I wrote JUDITH WAS TOO! I tried to make my handwriting look different. I thought about how maybe years from now, some camper would read those two messages and not even realize they were written by the same person.

Then I capped my pen and stuck it into my back-pack. My trunk had already been carried out by some Crockett counselors. I took one last look at everything before I walked out of the cabin for the last time.

Everyone was waiting for me on the hill. I'd told them I needed to go to Solitary. Courtney had said she'd come with me, but I'd told her to stick around with the others in case she missed saying good-bye to someone. I wanted to be alone when I signed the wall.

"Katherine just left," Courtney announced when I walked up to them.

"Oh, darn, I wanted to give her a big hug!" I joked.

"She said she'd e-mail you the second she got home," Mei assured me.

Michelle and Alex walked up. "They're starting to load the bus," said Michelle, and my heart dropped all the way down to my toes. That meant I had to leave now.

"I hate this!" Courtney said, burying her face in her hands. "I'm going to cry all day today!"

Last night had been bad enough. We'd all cried our eyes out at the Circle Fire. How could camp be over already?

Everyone walked with me to the bus. A big crowd of people was standing around, and everyone was hugging and crying and saying good-bye. I hated all the good-byes. But I was glad that my parents weren't coming to pick me up. I'd watched Isabel's mom when she was saying good-bye to all of us. Isabel had cried, and that made us cry. Her mom looked so upset that her daughter was reacting to going home by bursting into tears.

One by one everyone stepped up to say good-bye to me. Alex hugged me—Alex the slave driver, who was always frowning at me. "I'm really proud of you," she said.

"Oh, shut up!" I blubbered at her. I could take her being strict. I couldn't take her being proud of me.

"Take care, sweetie," said Michelle, giving me a big, long hug. "I'll be thinking about you. Everything will be fine. Write me or call me if you ever need to talk." Her eyes were all teary when she let go of me.

Then Mei, Lauren, and Courtney said their good-byes. It was all a big blur. We hugged and cried and promised to keep in touch. I felt like my heart was breaking. These guys had seen me through my JD experiment, without ever really knowing it.

"I'm going to miss you so much!" sobbed Courtney.

"Maybe we can visit each other during the school year. All four of us," I said, wiping away tears.

Just as I was about to go up the steps, Amber ran

up and gave me a hug. "Thank you. You're my favorite poet," I told her.

"I'm so glad you were in my cabin this year," said Amber. "You made it the most fun summer I've ever had here." That should've made me feel good, but I wished we'd gotten to know each other better. At least we'd had fun together with the talent show. I was glad about that.

Finally I walked up the steps. All of the bus windows were down, and girls were hanging out of the windows, still waving good-bye. I took an empty seat in the middle on the left side, so I could still look out the window and see everyone.

Then I saw Natasha getting on the bus, and I waved at her to come to my seat. "You can sit here. I promise I'll behave myself, and I won't sing any songs."

Natasha grinned as she put her stuff in the overhead bin and sat down. "I was hoping you'd sing 'Camp Days' for me!"

"Oh, that! I meant I wouldn't sing 'A Hundred Bottles of Beer on the Wall.'"

"Well, I never got a chance to tell you what a great job you did in the talent show. I told everyone you were my first friend!"

"Really? Cool. I'm glad everyone liked it. But it was really a group effort."

The driver closed the doors and started the engine. Natasha and I both stood up and waved to everyone one more time. Courtney, Mei, and Lauren did a few dance steps for me before the bus started pulling away. All three of them were still crying.

"I had a great summer," I said to Natasha.

"Yeah, me too," she agreed.

Now that camp was over, who should I be when I got home? Should I go back to being Judith like nothing had ever happened? Or maybe be somebody else? When would I know for sure who I was?

The bus rumbled down the gravel road and then turned onto the highway. We still had a long trip ahead of us. But I knew my family would be waiting for me at the bus station, and they'd all be so happy to see me. Maybe even Justin would come with them this time.

"You think you'll come back next summer?" Natasha asked me.

"I hope so," I said. "But I don't know for sure." There were lots of things I didn't know for sure. I sat back in the seat and looked out the window.

Maybe someday I'd know all the answers. Maybe someday I'd know exactly who I was.

I'd just have to wait and see.

Don't miss a single camper's story—here's a sneak peek at Kelly's, in *Summer Camp Secrets: Pranked!*

Sunday, June 15

This was definitely going to be the worst summer of my life.

I got out of the car and looked at all the people swarming around. It was mostly parents, but there were some other girls too, and even some brothers who looked as thrilled as I was to be here. Everyone was carrying something, and everyone seemed to know what to do and where to go. Except for us.

I just stood there holding my pillow. Then this woman who seemed to be in charge walked up. She had on a green polo shirt with a little pine tree on it. "I'm Eda Thompson, the camp director. Welcome to Pine Haven!"

My mom smiled with relief, and the two of them

started talking. Dad tried to wink at me, but I acted like I had to scratch my knee.

"This is our daughter, Kelly," my mom said.

"Hi, Kelly." The director smiled at me, then checked her clipboard. "Kelly Hedges, right? And you're twelve?"

I said yes, but it came out all croaky. I cleared my throat. "That's right."

She probably thought I didn't look twelve because I'm so vertically challenged. The director walked over to a group of people wearing green polos just like hers and motioned one of them to follow her back to us.

"This is Rachel Hoffstedder, and she's your counselor." Rachel shook hands with Mom and Dad, and then she shook my hand. She looked okay. She had really short dark brown hair, and she seemed friendly. And she was pretty vertically challenged herself. "Rachel will take you to your cabin." Then the director left to say hello to some other unhappy campers.

"Our cabin's that way." Rachel pointed up a steep hill. I could kind of see some cabins at the top of the hill, hidden in a bunch of trees. My dad was trying to wrestle my new metallic blue trunk out of the back of the car. The website had said we needed trunks to keep all our stuff in because there wasn't any place to store luggage.

"Why don't I get this end?" Rachel grabbed one of the trunk handles before my dad made a complete idiot of himself. Mom had my sleeping bag and tennis racket. I didn't have anything to carry but my pillow, which was better than nothing. At least it gave me something to hold on to.

We passed a bunch of other campers and parents going up the hill. I could tell some of them were really nervous. But then a lot of them acted like old friends. Girls kept shrieking at each other and hugging. It was beyond stupid to watch. I tried to relax my face and look casual, but my heart was pounding so hard I could feel the pulse in my throat.

What was I thinking when I agreed to this? Did they hypnotize me? Was it one of those weird parental mind control things? How had my parents ever talked me into spending a month at summer camp?

They started talking about camp back in March. They showed me the brochure and the website, and at that time it looked pretty cool. *Camp Pine Haven for Girls, located in the scenic mountains of North Carolina. A camping tradition since 1921.* Anyway, my best friend, Amanda, was going to be in Hawaii for two weeks, lying on a beach surrounded by a hundred gorgeous surfers. I figured she could miss me for two weeks after she got back from her dream vacation. In March camp seemed like a good idea. But that was March.

We walked up a dirt path and came to this big stone building with a porch. "That's Middler Lodge," said Rachel, and then we turned up another path and climbed a bunch of stone steps that went up yet another hill. There sure were lots of hills. My dad tried desperately not to pant, because Rachel wasn't breathing hard at all. She'd told us she was on the hiking staff, so she probably walked about thirty miles a day or something.

By now we were finally at the top of the hill where all the cabins were. There was a really wide dirt path, and all down one side was a long row of cabins. "This is Middler Line, and we're in Cabin 1A. You guys are in the middle between the Juniors—the little kids—and the Seniors—the oldest girls."

Rachel pushed open the screen door of the first cabin we came to, and she and my dad stumbled in and plopped my trunk on the floor. They each took a big breath.

"How many girls in each cabin again?" asked Mom.

"Eight, with two counselors. This is 1A, Kelly, and that's 1B." She waved to the left side of the cabin.

"You're number one! You're number one!" Dad

chanted. I wanted to hit him with my pillow, but I just looked around at everything.

Rachel laughed at his stupid joke, then spread out her arms. "Well, here it is. Your home away from home."

I'd seen the cabins in pictures on the website, but that didn't really give me an accurate view. I wouldn't be surprised if this cabin was built in 1921. It was all gray wood. The top half of the front and back walls were really just screens. The ceiling had wood beams across it with a couple of bare lightbulbs hanging down from them. But the weirdest thing was that there was graffiti *all* over the walls. Everywhere you looked, you could see where someone had written her name. There wasn't a blank space of wall anywhere. The website had called the cabins "rustic." "Primitive" was more like it.

"You're the first one here, so you get your choice of beds. This is mine, of course." Rachel pointed to a made-up cot against the wall. I had my choice of one set of bunk beds or two single cots next to them. They all looked uncomfortable. "The bottom bunk has extra shelf space. That's always a plus."

"Okay." I dropped my pillow on the bed.

"Let's get your bed made," said Mom. Rachel and my dad stood around looking useless, and I wandered toward the other side of the cabin, which was also full of empty bunks. And then I noticed something.

"Ah, excuse me, but . . . where's the bathroom?"

"They're not in the cabins. They're in another building down the line."

"You're kidding." I crossed my arms and glared at my dad. At home we didn't have to hike to the bathroom.

"Oh, it's not that bad." Dad tried not to smile. "It's like a college dorm. Let's see the rest of camp before your mom and I take off."

Just then another counselor and camper came in. Rachel helped them with all the stuff they were carrying. Then she introduced the counselor in 1B, Andrea Tisdale, who she said was a CA—a Counselor Assistant. I'm sure Mom and Dad were glad I didn't get her, because she was, like, in training or something. She said her activity was tennis. She was a lot taller than Rachel, and her long blond hair was in a ponytail.

As we were leaving, Andrea leaned over to Rachel and kind of whispered, "No sign of the Evil Twins yet, huh?"

Rachel laughed and shook her head. *Evil Twins?* What was that supposed to mean? My heart skipped three beats.

Rachel showed us the bathrooms. They were in

a building that looked kind of like the other cabins, except it was larger and had no screens. One side had a bunch of sinks, and the other side had a bunch of stalls. "This is 'Solitary.' And the showers are over there." She pointed to another building across from the bathrooms.

"Solitary?" I asked. I watched a granddaddy longlegs crawl down the wall of one stall.

Rachel smiled. "Yeah, that's what we call the bathrooms at Pine Haven."

"Why?" I mean, seriously. Why not just call it a bathroom?

"I'm not sure. Maybe because you're supposed to be by yourself but it's a communal toilet, so you're not really, or . . ." She just looked at me and shrugged.

Whatever. I know you're supposed to "rough it" at camp and all, but actually giving up private bathrooms, hair dryers, and air-conditioned houses with no crawly things—hey, this wasn't going to be easy. How long was I stuck here for? Four weeks—twenty-eight days. All right. Twenty-eight and counting.

After that Mom and Dad hung out for a while, looking at the camp. New campers were arriving all the time. I kept wondering about the *Evil Twins*. What was that all about? And were they in *my* cabin? The counselors had laughed about it, but that name didn't sound funny to me. I looked at all the strange faces around me. Who were the evil ones?

Then we heard a loud bell ringing—a real bell that a counselor was ringing by pulling a rope to make it clang.

"Lunchtime, Kelly. I'll see you in the dining hall," said Rachel.

Okay, so now my parents had to leave. My heart was beating about two hundred beats a minute. Dad gave me a bear hug and reminded me to write lots of long letters.

"We'll miss you so much!" said Mom. I could tell she was trying not to cry, which made me want to walk off without even saying good-bye.

"I'll be okay." My voice sounded like somebody else's. I hugged Mom really fast and then walked toward the dining hall without looking back. I could barely see it through the blur, but I blinked enough so that none of the tears rolled out.

Okay. So far, so good. I'd managed to say good-bye without crying. Much.